CHILDREN OF THE CIRCUS

Kenton Hall

Based on the AUK Studios Production
Children of the Circus
by Kenton Hall

and

The Greatest Show in the Galaxy
by Stephen Wyatt

Featuring Original Songs by Christopher Guard
with Additional Lyrics by Kenton Hall

Produced and Directed by Barnaby Eaton-Jones

This First Edition
Published in 2023 by
Oak Tree Books
oaktreebooks.uk

in association with
Chinbeard Books

Commissioning and Main Editor: Barnaby Eaton-Jones

Based on *The Greatest Show in the Galaxy* © 1988 Stephen Wyatt

Copyright © 2023 AUK Studios

Artwork/Design: Daniel McGachey
Original Layout/Typesetting: Kenton Hall

*This book is dedicated to a certain Time Lord
who, although they had to sit this adventure
out, was always there in spirit.*

Happy 60th Anniversary.

Contents

Cast

Christopher Guard as Bellboy
Dee Sadler as Flowerchild & Ella
Ian Reddington as Delios & Chief Clown
Sophie Aldred as Captain Gren & AJ
Sylvester McCoy as The High Poet
Toyah Wilcox as Mel'Dee & The Band

with
Barnaby Eaton-Jones
Kenton Hall
Kim Jones
Ian Kubiak

and featuring
Dean Hollingsworth as Bus Conductor & Announcer
Chris Jury as Deadbeat
Deborah Manship as Morgana
Jessica Martin as Mags
Daniel Peacock as Nord
Ricco Ross as The Ringmaster
Giann Sammarco as Whizz Kid

Special Vocal Performances by
Daisy Dunlop
Vanessa White

and special thanks to
Wink Taylor

Foreword

The Greatest Show in the Galaxy was first broadcast in 1988.

I never expected that it would still be remembered, discussed and (mostly) appreciated thirty-five years later. Still less that talented and apparently sane people would want to explore its world in their own creative projects.

Kenton has taken the characters and concepts from The Greatest Show into a new direction and come up with something weird, lyrical, scary and funny which is all his own. I particularly enjoyed the footnotes.

If I had written a sequel to The Greatest Show, it would have been nothing like Kenton's.

And that is exactly how it should be.

Stephen Wyatt

P.S. My most significant contribution to this project? They were going to call it *All Will Be Groovy*. I am glad that I persuaded them otherwise.

CHILDREN OF THE CIRCUS

Overture

The moment he saw the kites in the sky, he understood that there was no going back.

They circled above the pair of escapees like carrion birds, brightly painted on both sides and each featuring a large, unnerving eye symbol in their centre.

Two of them. More than enough.

The man knew the symbol well. Had learned to hate everything it represented. Yet, and this thought made him tired, it still conjured a feeling of home. The only real home he had ever known.

And from which he was now attempting to flee.

'Your kites,' he groaned to his companion. 'Your beautiful kites.'

Moments before, he had caught his foot on a rogue piece of scrub and tumbled heavily to the dusty track. He had briefly considered remaining there, allowing himself to be found, surrendering himself to his fate.

But the woman had knelt at his side and, as she had always done, lent him the strength to carry on.

It was something she clearly intended to keep doing.

'We mustn't think of that now!' she insisted. 'Come on!'

He turned to her. Almost smiled at his foolishness. Home was wherever she was. How could he ever think otherwise?

He straightened his shoulders, took his love's hand and prepared to run. If they were caught, so be it. At least they wouldn't have given up. They would live or die together.

And that was when they saw it.

A trail of fire across the sky.

Followed by an enormous explosion and a shower of dirt and debris.

Somewhere in the distance, between the sun-baked hills, a ship had crashed.

And nothing would ever be the same.

Chapter One

Encore Station.

It's a romantic name, isn't it? Evoking somewhere one might commemorate the end of a rollicking intergalactic adventure, rife with both derring and do. An oasis in which a weary space traveller could, conceivably, contemplate the stars, through generously proportioned viewing windows, and reflect on doomed love affairs between members of warring species. A cultural melting pot. An economic and social hub. An exotic elsewhere where one's best self might lurk.

Rick's Bar, basically, but with more airlocks and fewer Nazis.

And it *was* all that. And more.

Once.

If only you could have seen it then.

Let's start with the approach. This was a unique – or, if you were feeling cynical, eye-rollingly ostentatious – affair, celebrated in the folk ballads of a dozen disparate worlds.[1]

---

1. *When I First Espied Encore Station* being one of the most popular.

With most space stations, as you know, you simply drop out of hyperspace, or emerge from your favoured wormhole or vortex, then slow your engines and, following a brief subspace conflab about codes and procedures, cruise towards your designated docking port. A simple, robotic, bureaucratic process replicated across the known universe.

And far too boring for the like of Encore Station, which, conscious of its storied reputation, liked to put on a show.

There might have been an element of compensation at the core of this display. The structure itself did not appear especially remarkable at first glance: a large, slightly bulbous disc of burnished silver, bobbing gently within a faint blue energy shield and festooned with the usual clusters of antennae and gently blinking lights.

However, the moment *its* sensors picked up an arriving vessel, its systems would immediately and automatically perform a swift but thorough long distance scan, establishing not only the number of passengers and crew, but their names, ages, planets of origin, native and secondary languages and, where possible, beverage preferences.

The welcoming message each ship received, therefore, was highly personalised, wildly manipulative and, in terms of generating goodwill and, therefore, profit, extremely effective. It was, of course, also a security nightmare but there were few complaints. Encore Station was, after all, tucked away in a deserted corner of the galaxy and its visitors had often come a long way in cramped quarters.

If there were good vibes going, it was worth a little intrusion.

Besides, before they could think too deeply about it, a series of electronic buoys, arranged in long parallel lines between ship and station, would spark, one by one, into life. These had been cunningly and silently deployed as the ship's occupants boggled at the correct use of all eight of their formal matronymics and created a blazing corridor of light that led directly to their assigned airlock. Or, to quote the Encore Station Greeting Officer Training Manual (Vol. II) their 'home away from home'.

If anyone was foolish enough to believe that the sensory assault would diminish in intensity *inside* the station, they were soon disabused of the notion. As large, circular hydraulic doors whooshed shut behind them and they stepped out onto the long, broad central walkway leading into Encore proper, they were immediately assailed by a roar of noise and several competing spectrums' worth of light and colour.

Merchants bellowed out selections from their thrillingly obscure inventories, courtesy of the station-wide translation matrix. Children ran, fought, laughed, fell, flew in some cases, as weary parents issued ignored decrees from a safe distance. Travellers of every stripe – including, inevitably, those with actual stripes – scanned the bulkheads for signs of their next departure point. Lovers embraced in convenient shadows, specially constructed for the purpose. Musicians played unlikely instruments with confidence and flair.

A thick air of possibility – no doubt partly attributable to the state-of-the-art environmental controls – dominated the entire enterprise.

It was, to put it mildly, extraordinary.

But then stuff happened, the way stuff does.[2] And time passed, the way it's meant to but doesn't always. Entropy rocked up, without luggage or ready cash, and gave every indication that it planned to stick around for the foreseeable.

Before long, Encore Station had been irretrievably diminished. The merchants fled. The musicians got proper jobs, with pensions and sociable working hours. The lovers decided they needed space to get their heads together.

And, finally, only the lost remained.

*

There had been no sensor sweep of the barely space-worthy freighter on which Ella had made her way to Encore Station. And even if there had been, it would have been unlikely to detect the young stowaway, sandwiched as she had been, in the cargo hold, between crates of chrono-shielded, freeze-dried gumblejack. At best, she might have registered as somewhat lively for a dead fish, but not enough to motivate its overextended crew to investigate.

---

2. *Stuff* is used here in its most technical sense, as the collective noun for a collision of events slightly more devastating than adolescent heartbreak and slightly less so than your average Apocalypse. Some academics claim that this presents so subjective a definition as to be meaningless, but no one you've heard of.

Likewise, she had disembarked without issue, station security having been reduced to a single guard who had taken the job as a stopgap while they worked on their holo-screenplay.

She explored further now, each cautious step echoing metallically across the emptiness. Her gaze roamed, taking in her surroundings, clearly looking for *something*. Though even she couldn't have articulated precisely what that was.

Ella was a humanoid of youthful appearance and slightly less than average height.[3] Her thick, dark, wavy hair had been hacked, with little obvious care, into a ragged bob, convenience winning out over style. Her eyes, a steely blue, were those of someone who had packed significantly more experience into her years than recommended in the manual and were set in a face to whom genetics had briefly gifted softness and delicacy before life stomped in and repossessed the lot.

She stopped suddenly and fumbled in one pocket of her thick, padded jacket (worn above a pair of ill-fitting trousers that almost, but not quite, resembled an ancient Terran fabric known as denim).

'Where the hell is it?' she grunted, shifting her attention to the other pocket before finally locating what she was after.

'Ah hah!'

Ella drew out a slender rod of a substance that resembled polished onyx. A small dial was set into its

---

3. For a humanoid. To the inhabitants of Forgon IV, one of the few sentient races to exist at the microscopic level, she might as well have been a planet.

base; she twisted it and, after a moment and a sharp, impatient tap, the rod began to glow.

Then she held the device up to her ear and frowned in concentration, as though listening. As the rod did not appear to be emitting any audible sounds, it had the effect of making her appear, in the politest possible terms, reality adjacent.

'Yes,' she barked, reinforcing the impression, 'that's what you said the last thousand times. But I'm starting to think you've given me dodgy directions.'

Ella looked up. The handful of other people currently being disappointed by Encore Station averted their respective gazes. The place felt so abandoned that she'd almost forgotten she wasn't entirely alone.

'Sorry!' she called out, which didn't seem to help. 'Not dangerous or anything! Just confused!' she added, which helped even less.

There was a general exodus towards less worrying parts of the station, should they exist.

Ella sighed.

'Well done,' she chided herself. 'Making friends and influencing people as always.'

She noticed, however, that at least one person, at the other end of the walkway, hadn't run away in abject terror. They were wearing a one piece jumpsuit in a pale, official-looking grey and walked with purpose. Everything about them, or, more correctly, the back of them, screamed competence. They looked, to be precise, like a responsible adult.

Ella jogged towards them.

'Excuse me!' she called out.

Her fellow traveller did not respond. Or even turn around. But they didn't bolt either so Ella persisted, quickly catching up with them.

'Excuse me,' she repeated, 'I'm really sorry, but... could I just ask...'

This time, their quarry did turn. And, for a brief moment, it was Ella who was tempted to flee. Not wishing to be rude, however, she restricted herself to:

'Oh. Oh, wow.'

'We are sorry,' came the reply, 'we were... thinking.'

The voice attached to this statement was unusual in that, unlike Ella, it did not travel alone. She was certain she could hear at least four distinct voices in the mix, swirling over and around each other, synchronous but, somehow, jostling for prominence.

Their tone was flat and calm. So utterly calm that it put Ella's nerves on edge.

'And why wouldn't you be?' she blurted, trying to cover for her inadvertent *faux pas.* 'Thinking, I mean. We've all got to think somewhere.'

She felt deeply embarrassed and, worse, like a rube.[4] A seasoned space traveller was meant to be inured to difference.

Ella wished she was a seasoned space traveller. Or, in this moment at least, less of an idiot.

'You are disturbed by our appearance.' It was not an accusation, it seemed, merely a statement, but it stung. Mostly because it was true. The voice, striking as it was, had some competition.

---

4. Here meaning 'uncultured bumpkin' rather than the carnivorous shrubs native to Xerxes III.

'No.'

'Ah, you are a liar,' they observed. 'No matter. We are used to dissemblance.'

Ella felt a surge of annoyance. Okay, so she clearly wasn't making the best first impression. But did that mean she had to stand for being insulted?

'Whoah there. Back up a minute. I am *not* a liar.'

Her confidence ebbed as quickly as it had flowed.

'All right, I did lie *a bit* just then but I was trying to be kind.'

She received a small shrug in return.

'We have been made similar assurances in the past. It is of no consequence.'

'Look, I'm sorry. You just...'

'Ask.'

'What?'

'Ask. We are happy to explain.'

Ella blinked. That didn't seem like a good idea *at all*.

'No, I don't think...'

'ASK.'

There was a hint of frustration, even anger, in this last demand which, oddly, made Ella feel more comfortable.

'Fine,' she said. 'What is going on with your face?'

'Ah, our face. What about it? Specifically.'

Again, the voices were even but positively dripping with meaning. This was obviously not the first time they'd come up against insensitivity or prejudice; Ella felt a wave of sadness wash over her. She wouldn't pretend to understand exactly what they'd been through but she knew what it was to feel the unremitting pressure to *explain* yourself.

All right then, she thought. In for a Graxian pnar, in for a Graxian piq'pnar.

'It keeps changing.'

And that was the salient point. Like the voice, her new acquaintance's face and, indeed, the rest of their body, appeared to have four variants, but instead of appearing simultaneously, they were in constant flux.

'Yes.'

'Like it can't settle on what you're supposed to look like.'

'We can see how you might reach that conclusion.'

'You a shapeshifter?'

'No.'

'Hologram?'

'No.'

'Did I eat something funny? Because, if I'm honest, the options have been a bit limited.'

The voices headed off any further guesses.

'We are The Band of Infinite Harmony.'

'Of course. That explains it.'

'Does it?'

'Not in the slightest.'

'We were four. We are now one. It is... difficult to explain.'

Ella felt a sudden urge to hug this Band of Infinite Harmony, whatever that may turn out to mean.

'I'll bet. But I suppose you don't end up at Encore Station unless you've seen a few difficult to explain things.'

Or, she added to herself, unless you've ended up entirely out of your element on what amounted to a whim.

'You chased us down.'

'What?'

'You approached us. You had a question?'

'Yes!' Ella grabbed gratefully at the conversational lifeline. 'Yes, I did! Though I'm after directions, really.'

The Band stared back impassively, waiting for Ella to expand on this. Still, a little transfixed by the shifting faces, it took her a moment.

Four voices coughed, in harmony.

'Right,' said Ella. 'Yes.'

She held up the little black rod and twisted the dial again. Then she swept her thumb up the length of the device, causing a trail of soft, orange light to appear.

'You see, I received this about a month ago.'

The rod crackled and a recording began to play, this time perceptible to all.

It was a deep, mellifluous voice with a certain music to it. It inspired, in Ella at least, a touch of melancholy.

'Ella,' it said. 'The survivors of the Circus must unite. Come to Encore Station. All will be explained.'

Ella twisted the dial again and the rod powered down.

'I'm Ella,' she added. 'For the sake of clarity.'

The Band, for the first time, seemed genuinely taken aback.

'And you are a survivor of the Circus?'

She shook her head.

'That's the thing. I'm pretty sure I'm not. I've survived a *lot*, don't get me wrong, but I don't

12

remember a circus in the mix. And, unless it was a very boring circus, I think I would.'

'Then why did you come?'

An excellent question, thought Ella. She wished she had a better answer.

'I was at something of a loose end. Also, it was addressed to me, which I thought was weird enough to warrant further investigation.'

'Why was this... weird?'

Ella couldn't suppress a slight grin. She held up the device again.

'This is not *my* communicator. Well, it wasn't, anyway. I lifted it off a security guard on Anura who wouldn't keep his flippers to himself.'

'You are a thief.'

'Maybe. But still not a liar. Anyway, it's taken me the best part of a month to get here, courtesy of some of the galaxy's best and smelliest cargo holds. A month of wondering what the hell I was about to walk into. And I have to say, I was expecting something more... dramatic.'

The Band hesitated briefly, then replied, softly.

'As were we.'

Ella clapped her hands.

'See? I knew I stopped the right person... or, rather, people. You *are* survivors of this circus, whatever it is?'

'We are.'

'Brilliant. So, any idea what this is all about?'

'No.'

'One step forward, two steps back. Never mind. But you do know where to go? You seemed like you were heading somewhere specific.'

'We do. We were.'

'Where?'

The Band turned on their heel and began to stride away.

'Follow us,' they said.

*

Reaching the end of the walkway, they made their way down a series of the sort of long, tight corridors that make submarine holos so exhausting. Ella was grateful, possibly for the first time ever, for a childhood spent largely in enclosed spaces. The Band barely seemed to notice.

At the end of the final corridor was a hatch. Like all other doors on the station, it was big and round and constructed of a thick, dull metal that promised you would only get past it on its own terms.

Still, as they approached, it hissed open and they passed through into a much larger, more open space. It was more populated too. Not the Encore of old, but decidedly less abandoned.

The room was built into the curve of the station, its exterior wall set with large transparent panels, beyond which the vast expanse of space loomed.

In front of this, competing with the view, a makeshift stage had been erected; audio-bots hovered in each corner, ready to broadcast whatever was about to take place.

There was expectation in the air, that much was certain. It radiated from each of the dozen or so isolated groups that had gathered around the room.

Ella took a moment to let it wash over her. Having never seen Encore in its pomp, she was impressed by how many species were represented.

'Okay, this is more like it!'

'More like what?' asked The Band.

'I don't know,' Ella admitted, struggling to articulate the fluttering sensation growing in her gut. Maybe she had eaten something untoward after all. 'Something more in keeping with mysterious messages and abandoned space stations.'

But The Band were now taking their turn to fixate on the crowd.

'There are so... few.'

'What do you mean? I'd have said it was a pretty good crowd. And from all over the galaxy as well, from the looks of it. I mean, isn't that a Haroovian Priestess over there?'

The Band followed Ella's outstretched finger. It was true. No one else in the galaxy wore gowns of that particular shade of luminescent yellow. Or had as many elbows.

'When's the last time anyone saw a Haroovian Priestess outside of a museum?' Ella continued, still marvelling.

'You don't understand,' The Band offered, without rancour. 'There were so many lost.'

'Oh,' said Ella, the implication of the word *survivors* finally sliding into place. 'I didn't think. I'm so sorry.'

'You were not to know.'

'But I *want* to know.'

'We are not certain that is true.'

'I think I might need to. What the hell is this? And what does it have to do with a circus?'

As if in answer, a thunderous chord of music filled the room.[5] It rolled out over the audience like a storm cloud, dragging voices in its wake. Voices that Ella knew, without being told, belonged to the past.

First, a soft mumble.

'Shadows fall ever behind, when faces confront sun.'

Then a more aggressive voice, almost a growl.

'I know what it is to be trapped. I know how hard it is to fight to be yourself. To fight *against* yourself. To the death. Against blood, tradition, darkness. All those things that the Circus came to represent.'

Ella felt a chill clamber up her spine. There was something morbid about these disembodied voices. It felt somehow wrong to be listening to them, as if she was eavesdropping.

A woman with an unlikely accent – that she abandoned halfway through her first sentence – was next.

'The early days, that's what I try to hold onto. Finding our way, finding ourselves.'

'I know these voices,' whispered The Band.

'Is that a good or bad thing?'

Slowly, a melody began to develop beneath the... testimony was the word, Ella decided. It took the initial

---

5. Audio-bot broadcasts are something akin to the Terran concept of surround sound but in addition to immersing *you* in the *sound*, they immerse the *sound* in *you*. Refreshments are seldom served at audio-bot supported concerts and with good reason.

chord and built on it, adding nuance and movement. It was achingly sad.

A man who sounded as if he absolutely, one hundred percent, owned more than one pair of sandals offered some wisdom:

'It's all part of the healing process. So, yeah, that's what I want for them all. Don't forget. Don't forgive, even. But don't let the Circus define you.'

And then, incongruously, a blast of spoken verse:

> *If you think you'll catch me out*
> *To take blame for the final bout*
> *I'm afraid you're out of luck*
> *The past ain't where this man is stuck*

The phrase *tonal inconsistency* leapt, unbidden, into Ella's mind.[6]

Before she could regroup, a darker, more angular chord struck like a viper, an atonal wail burrowing through its centre. The voices began to come faster and with more force, talking over each other like a series of one-sided arguments.

'And I told you, I'm not interested in talking. I don't care who you say you are. Now get out before I do something unspeakable to your nostrils.'

'Enough questions! Tickets please!'

---

6. In some galactic cultures, it became briefly popular for art critics to broadcast psychically, on the grounds that no one was listening to them anymore. This was controversial in the extreme and almost destroyed the entertainment industries of more than one planet. Not to mention the number of altercations and subsequent lawsuits occasioned by people suddenly shouting '*mise en scene*' at each other for no reason.

'No, no, you've got it all wrong. That's not what the Circus is about *at all*. Let me guess, you're a *new* fan.'

'We all did what we had to do. It's not like I was *enjoying* myself. If you think you can do better with... whatever you have planned, knock yourself out. It's all the same to me.'

The music was *angry* now. It seethed and slithered and twisted. Ella wrapped her arms protectively around her chest and noticed, from the corner of her eye, that The Band had done the same.

It clawed and screamed to a climax and then...

All was quiet.

Too quiet, as the saying goes.

But then another voice. Singular. Present.

'Survivors of the Circus,' it said, enunciating the capital 'C' of Circus with precision. 'I welcome you.'

The voice belonged, it seemed, to the figure who had just stepped out onto the stage. A man in a braided yellow military jacket over purple bell-bottomed trousers.

'Impossible,' breathed The Band.

'What the hell is he wearing?' asked Ella.

'What he always wore.'

'You used to be in a marching band together, I take it.'

The man continued to speak, pacing slowly up and down the front of the stage, his voice thickened by emotion. His half smile and gentle tone reminded Ella a little of the priests that used to visit the workers' quarters on special occasions.

But significantly less creepy.

18

'I can tell from the looks on your faces that some of you know me as well as I know *all* of you. My fellow travellers. Across decades and light years. From the peaks of joy to the depths of sorrow.'

'But it cannot be him,' said The Band.

'Cannot be who?'

'He was lost.'

'Looks pretty found to me.'

'You do not understand.'

'You got that right.'

The man stopped centre-stage and opened his arms, as if proffering an embrace.

'And I know what many of you are thinking. What I would be thinking, were I stood in your place.'

He paused for effect.

'Didn't I die?'

The audience, which up until this point had adopted a stunned silence, began to murmur once more.

'Hey,' said Ella, struck by a realisation. 'The voice on my communicator. It's him!'

She turned to The Band. Each of their faces, in turn, had drained of blood. Another thought came charging in behind.

'But you knew that, didn't you? You recognised his voice.'

'We did not believe it could be true.'

'Because he's supposed to be dead? Lots of people are *supposed* to be dead. They're the ones who never are.'

'Please, be quiet. You do not grasp what is occurring here.'

'Do you?'

The man was smiling now. It was somehow comforting and terrifying in equal measure.

'Let me assure you. Reports of my death have been wholly... accurate.'

There were a few gasps, a couple of oddly translated curses and the sound of at least one person hitting the deck in a dead faint. Fear, which, to be honest, had been standing at the door waving for a while, began to creep in.

'I, like so many of those not with us today, our friends and family, was a victim of the Psychic Circus. My life – my love – taken from me for the amusement and appeasement of cruel and sybaritic Gods.'

'Sorry, what?' asked Ella.

The Band's voices dipped to a hoarse undertone.

'The Gods. The Gods of Ragnarok.'

Ella considered this new piece of information for a moment then sighed.

'I never get invited to anything *nice.*'

'We few, we sorrowful few, we band of happy accidents, are very nearly all that has survived,' intoned the man, as music once more began to play, 'You heard, just now, from a handful of others, scattered across the stars. Some have moved on, found new paths, even tried to resurrect the Circus as something pure... but too many still live in that darkness. Our bodies may have fled or been abandoned, but our souls...'

This time, there was a beat. A solid downbeat, clockwork-tight, punctuating the punchline.

'...they never left the Circus.'

And, then, in a move that really shouldn't have surprised anyone at that point, Bellboy began to sing.

*

How do you describe a song?

There are those who maintain it can't be done. What's more, they insist, it shouldn't be done. You don't dance about architecture. You don't knit about yodelling. Why the hell should you write about music? Art is designed to be felt, not transmuted.

Others, of course, make their livings and reputations describing songs, albeit concentrating heavily on why they aren't as good as previous songs that they've heard.

Consider this the middle ground.

Bellboy's song was rousing but nuanced. Epic but personal. A call to arms, if those arms had been gently flung around you as an act of comfort.

In it, he explained that he knew what they were going through. That he too had suffered as they had suffered. That he *understood*.

In the chorus, as one must, he switched things up. Time was not inflexible. The past could be changed. Their fates could be reversed. They were all residents, not of what was, but what *used to be*.

It was a promise. A vow.

And catchy as hell.

*

To say that Bellboy didn't expect the muted response he received to his melodious plea would be

21

disingenuous. He expected it plenty. These weren't – as his little highlights reel bore out – the first survivors who hadn't bought what he was selling. But it was the biggest crowd he'd played to, the first time he'd been able to gather so many of the fallen together in one place. And, despite knowing better, he had let himself hope.

At the edge of the stage, the final notes still drifting into silence, he had addressed them with all the passion at his disposal.

'Our pasts. Our losses. Our pain. They can all be changed. I stand here before you as evidence that what *was* need not be what *is*. And I'm asking you to join me in rewriting the past. I have found the technology. I have laid out the plans. Let us take back, together, what the Circus took from us.'

Bellboy watched with dismay as the crowd, too afraid of the implications of what they'd heard to do otherwise, began to edge towards the exits. Crazy Dead Guy Wants to Do Time Travel was not, clearly, what anyone considered to be a safe bet.

He called out after them.

'Please, I assure you. I know it seems fantastical, but this can be done. And don't we owe it to ourselves, to those we lost, to try?'

The answer, if the swiftly emptied room was to be believed, was no.

Ella turned to The Band. They had not moved an inch.

'That was painful to watch,' she said.

'He... speaks the truth.'

'He speaks like he's nursing an untreated head wound. And what was with the singing?'

'A song is a powerful thing.'

'Look, I bounce a tune around the sonic shower same as everyone else, but even the most killer chorus has never motivated me to attempt a wholesale rewrite of time.'

'Until now.'

Ella frowned.

'What do you mean?'

The Band fixed her with a look that used up all four faces.

'You are still here. Everyone else is leaving.'

'You're not.'

'No. We are not.'

'You believe this guy?'

'We wish to. We need to. As, we suspect, do you.'

Ella shook her head.

'Why would I? I'm only here out of morbid curiosity. I'd never even heard of – what did he call it? – the Psychic Circus until I received that ridiculous invitation.'

'You have a past. As do we all. And you wish to know if you are... stuck with it.'

'Aargh!'

'Aargh?'

'Four minds against one isn't fair. You know that right?'

At least one of The Band's faces smirked; Ella would have sworn to it.

'We will seek out Bellboy.'

'He's called *Bellboy*?'

'On my homeworld, *Ella* is a disease of the foot.'

'Fine. But when they write my obituary, please have them say that I hesitated a little? So I don't seem like a complete idiot?'

'This seems a fair request.'

'Thank you.'

'We have one question.'

'Yes?'

'What is an obituary?'

Ella nudged her new friends towards the exit.

'A story with a sensible ending,' she muttered.

Chapter Two

Bellboy stormed down the corridor, cursing under his breath. He was not in good mood. Not that he had ever had a reputation for being the life of the party. He was an engineer, after all. He built and fixed things. People came pre-built and could seldom be fixed, rendering them, therefore, confusing. He was also highly intelligent, detail-orientated and shy, a combination which is often mistaken for solipsistic.

But that was why he and Flowerchild had been perfect for one another. She liked people, understood people, and when they'd been together, Bellboy had liked and understood people too. Since they'd been apart, he had tried to live the way she would have wanted him to. With people.

It was a challenge. His heart was broken and no one seemed willing to help him mend it.

'The fools!' he said, as much to himself as to the slender, timid man at his side. 'I offer them a chance to change their own histories. To eliminate their pain. And they... shrug, basically.'

Delios of Othrys raised his watery eyes briefly, before almost immediately returning his gaze to the deck. He had a shock of untidy brown hair and was wearing the traditional robe of a Poet of Othrys. It looked comfortable enough, cozy even, but was at least two sizes too big.

All the better to hide in.

'The clarion call did not ring out,' he murmured.

Bellboy waved a hand apologetically, the random phrase seemingly making perfect sense to him.

'I know. I was going to bring you out as a sort of grace note. But we'd already lost them.'

Delios stopped in his tracks, like a sullen child.

'A citadel upon a hill. Silent, steady, calm and still.'

Bellboy felt the warm glow of temper begin to build beneath his ribcage. He tried his best to tamp it down but he could hear it in his reply.

'Delios, I *know*. And you're right, maybe I could have brought them round. But we're, ironically, running out of time.'

Bellboy and Delios had been together for what felt like eons – since almost the beginning of this struggling enterprise. And most of the time, they rubbed along just fine. Delios had, after all, been the first survivor to believe Bellboy, to join his crusade. But Delios was also a poet and, like most poets, often insufferable. He didn't mean to be, it was just a side effect. Like starship captains being romantically incontinent. Or desert-dwelling species saying: 'That hits the spot!' after every single sip of water.

'From these lips. Twisted by fire.'

26

Bellboy heard the tremor of anxiety in Delios' voice and softened his tone.

'No, old friend. We're not giving up. And you will be whole again. We all will. We'll just have to take a more ragtag approach.'

He laid an encouraging hand on the poet's shoulder.

'Come on. Let's get back to the ship.'

*

'Okay, so let me get this straight. The Circus itself was psychic?'

'Not as such.'

'Then you had a lot of psychics on staff?'

'During our tenure?'

'Yes.'

'No.'

'Then why call it the Psychic Circus?'

'We did not name it.'

'Sounds like a marketing ploy to me.'

'Perhaps.'

There had been very little detective work involved in tracking down the docking port from which Bellboy and company would be departing. For starters, there was the matter of the stage. Apparently, it – along with some other rather unusual looking machinery – belonged not to the station but to the performer, so it was easy enough to pry the location out of the half dozen irritable workers assigned to disassemble and deliver it back to them.

Not that even this proved necessary. Ella and The Band had – on the time-honoured grounds that it was worth a shot – simply waited outside the backstage area and followed them home. They hadn't even really kept much of a distance.

They had certainly overheard much of what had been said *en route*. It had mostly confused Ella further but had caused The Band to fall even more silent and pensive. Which was why Ella had taken it upon herself to keep asking questions. In her experience, if you couldn't snap someone out of a mood, the only remaining option was to annoy them into a different one.

So far, it was working. The Band were definitely annoyed.

'It's suspect. That's all I'm saying.'

'Stop.'

'Calm down. I'm only making conversation.'

'No, stop walking. We believe we have arrived.'

Just ahead of them, Bellboy and Delios had turned a corner into the main docking area. The Band began to follow, but Ella held up her hand.

'Hang back a minute. Let them get comfortable.'

*

Bellboy flipped open a small keypad next to the docking hatch and began to enter his security code.[7] Two numbers in, he paused and looked back over his shoulder at Delios.

'Gren isn't going to be happy.'

Delios shrugged.

_____

7. In keeping with the lax nature of the modern Encore Station, it was 0000.

'The clock unchanged sits – hours, seconds, face.'

'No, I suppose she isn't. But she was looking forward to some help around the ship.'

'A better cue line I've yet to hear,' came a voice from a nearby corridor.

Bellboy and Delios both pretended not to have been startled and turned to see who had spoken.

Ella gave a little wave.

'Hiya!'

Delios seemed unperturbed by the new arrivals. In that he looked no more miserable than previously.

But Bellboy's jaw had dropped. His eyes had taken on the fine glaze of a well-prepared ham. His arms hung limply at his sides.

'Flowerchild?'

It was an uncanny resemblance, thought Bellboy. The hair was wrong, of course, and the eye colour and Flowerchild would never have been caught wearing anything so *functional*. But other than that, they were identical.

'I think,' said Ella, 'we'll lay off the pet names until we've been properly introduced. *Bellboy.* Your parents didn't want children, I take it.'

'I'm sorry. For a moment, you... No. My apologies. It has been a long day.'

'Can you do what you claim?' asked The Band, cutting across the mood.

Bellboy looked at The Band. To Ella's chagrin, he didn't even flinch. *That* is how a seasoned space traveller behaves, she thought.

'Yes,' he said plainly.

Delios backed him up.

'No falsehood rests here. Its sleep would be disturbed by the dawn's insistent light.'

Bellboy stepped to one side and presented his friend with a small flourish.

'You never met Delios of Othrys, did you?'

'No,' said The Band, 'He served before our time. But it is our honour.'

Delios inclined his head shyly.

'Honour raises a hand, but never to strike.'

'He says likewise,' Bellboy translated. 'And, may I add how good it is to see *you* again. I had hoped you'd come.'

'We are... glad you are not dead.'

'Thank you. That's very kind. Almost makes me wish it were true.'

'Sorry to break up the class reunion,' interjected Ella, a little irritated at losing the focus of the group so quickly, 'but my name's Ella. We *haven't* met but I received one of your little save-the-date broadcasts and I want to know why.'

Bellboy pursed his lips.

'I don't recognise the name. When did you travel with the Circus?'

'I didn't.'

'In that case, consider yourself lucky and get as far away from here as possible.'

'If I had anywhere else to go, would I come here?'

The Band stepped forward.

'Bellboy, we believe the young woman may have been drawn here for a purpose.'

Bellboy seemed to hesitate for a moment and The Band was fairly sure they knew why.

'And on what are you basing that theory?' he asked, finally.

'She is here. Others are not.'

'Can't argue with that. All right. I take it the cause has two new willing volunteers?'

'I'm not here for any cause,' said Ella. 'I just want to know why I'm here.'

'I'd be careful, throwing around the big questions like that,' said Bellboy, with a nod in Delios' direction. 'You might set him off. Still, you're right, we should get to the bottom of why you were invited.'

'It was *your* voice on the recording.'

'Which I don't remember sending. Although I'm learning that time travel tends to throw up these little anomalies. And I did... delegate some of the research.'

'To whom?' enquired The Band.

Bellboy punched the final two numbers into the keypad.

'I think it's time you met our crew.'

Chapter Three

The Starship Vanguard[8] was a vessel with a storied history. Which is to say, there were many stories told about its history. Some of which were even true.

But not many.

It had been the final craft built at the legendary shipyards of Estigon, some said. It contained within its navigational mainframe the secret location of any number of lost treasures, from the Sierra Madre to Sierra Prime. It was powered by the essence of an imprisoned Eternal.

It did not exist at all and anyone who said otherwise was a sheep in thrall to the Galactic Authority.

What all of the stories had in common was their source.

The Captain of the Starship Vanguard.

Their name was Gren and they were justly legendary.

Hailing from the forest planet of Hyrax, they were also approximately four feet tall, covered head to toe

---

8. Named, of course, for its designer, Horatio Van Guard.

in a green bark-like substance and suffered fools about as gladly as they suffered everyone else.

*

'And what, precisely, do you expect me to do about it?' they said now, clutching the arms of their command chair as an alternative to launching anything heavy in the direction of their navigator.

'I didn't say there *was* anything you could do about it.'

AJ *was* that navigator and she and Gren had been together for longer than anyone cared to remember. The bickering had started a week later than that. In truth, they loved each other deeply. So much so that it was ceaselessly surprising to those who knew them both that either of them had survived this long.

The bridge of the Vanguard had not been constructed along the sleek lines that the general populace had come to expect from a starship of its fighting weight. Sure there were panels and buttons and blinking lights aplenty, but there was also a fair amount of moss and, for some reason, an overwhelming aroma of burnt toast.

It had, Gren maintained, a *lived-in* look.

'You can't leave the ship,' they reminded AJ, knowing from the first word that it was a mistake.

'I know that, Captain.' AJ had the sort of voice that people insist on describing as 'bubbly' when what they actually mean is 'infuriating'.

'So what's the point of telling me that I never take you anywhere?'

'Because it's how I *feel*. Don't you want to know how I feel?'

Gren ground their teeth together in frustration, which in a wood-based species classified as a fire hazard.

'I would love,' they said, 'for even five minutes, to be remotely in the dark about how you feel.'

'Well, that's a wonderful attitude.'

The whoosh of the bridge's door opening made Gren sigh with relief. They spun in their chair, expecting to see Bellboy and Delios and ready with a witticism about the failure of their latest recruitment attempt. To their credit, they barely reacted to the additional presence of Ella and The Band.

'That was quick,' they said, dryly.[9]

'Go on,' said Bellboy. 'Get it out of your system.'

'Look,' replied Gren, 'just because I told you – repeatedly – that not everyone was going to leap at the chance to join your lunatic crusade, doesn't mean I'm going to gloat about it.'

'Gracious of you.'

'A word unspoken may wound as deeply as a scream,' observed Delios.

'Granted,' said Gren, waving dismissively. 'But I am absolutely without opinion on the subject. No judgement here *at all*.'

Bellboy waited patiently.

'Although I did tell you *repeatedly*.'

There it was.

'I'm sorry, Bellboy,' chimed in AJ.

---

9. Also a fire hazard.

34

'Thank you. But I think it's for the best. We're still on track, after all. And who knows? There may be other opportunities.'

'Besides,' said Gren, focusing their attention on the newcomers, 'my money was on *nobody*. Care to introduce me to your new friends?'

'Old friends, in some cases. This is... The Band of Infinite Harmony.'

'Oh, fantastic!' chirped AJ. 'I so hoped I'd have an opportunity to meet you. Your file was *so* interesting. Welcome aboard!'

'You are most kind,' said The Band.

'And this is Ella,' added Bellboy pointedly. 'AJ, I don't suppose you want to fill us in on why *she's* here?'

'No idea.'

'She was invited.'

'Not by me.'

'Nor me.'

'That seems unlikely.'

'Yes. Yes, it does.'

'Excuse me,' interrupted Ella.

'What is it?' asked Gren.

'At the risk of seeming terribly rude... who are you talking to?'

'My apologies,' said Bellboy. 'This is Captain Gren. Owner and operator of the Starship Vanguard.'

'Captain,' nodded Ella. 'Nice place you've got here, et cetera, but I think you know who I'm asking about.'

'Ah,' said Bellboy, 'AJ.'

'If you say so.'

'AJ is the ship's navigator.'

'That,' offered AJ sniffily, 'is a gross simplification.'

Ella stepped forward, eyes scanning the bridge. She addressed, for lack of a better option, the air.

'AJ, I don't know quite how to put this but... are you invisible?'

'No,' came the firm reply. 'Although sometimes it *feels* like I am.'

Gren sighed.

'Don't start.'

'Unseen. Unfelt. Unknown. Yet dwelt,' Delios posited.

'And you're welcome to take a breather as well.'

Ella ignored them all.

'Are you speaking from another part of the ship?'

'Also, no.'

'Right,' Ella spun back to face the rest of the crew. 'Anyone want to chip in and rescue me here?'

The Band raised their hand.

'We may have a solution.'

'AJ is not the ship's computer,' said Bellboy.

'We do not have a solution.'

'Ignore them,' said AJ sweetly. 'It's perfectly natural to have questions. Go to the navigator's chair.'

Ella made her way down three short steps towards a large rectangular bank of controls that stretched across the bridge, facing the viewscreen. There was a seat at either end, both bolted to the deck.

'It's the one on the right.'

'Okay.'

'Feel free to have a seat!'

Ella sat.

'Look at the panel directly below the gyro controls.'

Ella did.

'You should see a small patch of rust.'

Ella looked. There *was* a small, squarish patch of rust. About three inches long and almost as wide.

'Yep.'

'Hello!'

And it had been going so well.

'You've lost me.'

'That's me,' said AJ. 'The patch of rust.'

Gren clambered from their chair and marched down the steps.

'She's showing off now. Basically, AJ is what happens when you retrofit a space vehicle for time travel on a budget.'

'Rust,' murmured Ella. 'Sentient rust.'

'A tiny little hiccup in the temporal shielding. That panel is seven billion years ahead of the rest of the ship. AJ isn't rust, she's the natural evolution of rust.'

This time, Gren sounded almost proud.

'If you wanted proof that we can actually travel in time,' said Bellboy, 'AJ is the best we've got.'

Ella ran her hands over her face.

'I think I might need a little lie down.'

'Precisely what I was going to suggest next,' replied Bellboy. 'Captain, permission to show our guests to their quarters?'

'Granted. Although, I hope they're not expecting much. The Vanguard is a fine ship, but it leans towards function, rather than form.'

'I spent the last week sleeping between crates of freeze-dried fish. My definition of luxury has grown extremely flexible.'

'A woman after my own heart.'

'Form is final's final form.'

'Delios, dear,' said Gren. 'Do me a nice quiet favour and see if you can sort out our next jump point. This little side jaunt to Encore has thrown all of my calculations out of whack.'

'Favour fortunes the bold.'

'Just so.'

'Captain,' complained AJ. 'I told you that I have that in hand.'

'I just thought a second pair of eyes might be useful.'

'Oh, nice. You know I don't have eyes.'

'You don't have hands either.'

Bellboy waved Ella towards the door.

'I think that's our cue.'

'We are in agreement,' added The Band.

Ella stumbled past the arguing captain and navigator. Everything was beginning to feel a little dream-like. Any minute now she'd find herself naked on stage, being asked to sing a Draconian aria she'd never learned.

'I'm genuinely just going with the flow at this point.'

Bellboy hit a panel and the door whooshed again.

'Oh, Bellboy,' called Captain Gren, before it could close behind them. 'Come back up here when you're done, will you? I think we need to talk next steps.

Chapter Four

'I take it this wasn't always a time ship,' said Ella, as they made their way down the corridor leading from the bridge. Gren's warnings about the Vanguard's utilitarian nature were accurate. Space was at a premium and a large number of rusty metal protrusions impinged on what there was.

'Why do you say that?' asked Bellboy, with genuine curiosity.

'The whole thing with AJ, for starters.'

'Ah, yes.'

'And it's kind of... what's the polite word?'

'Shopworn?'

'That's the one. It looks like it's been well and truly shopworn. Possibly with a mallet.'

Bellboy smiled.

'Gren used to be a smuggler. Somewhere along the line, they had the bright idea that they could avoid some unduly harsh penal sentences by delivering the goods before they were stolen.'

'Ingenious.'

'You'd be surprised the kind of upgrades you can get on the black market. You still sing beautifully, by the way.'

This last remark was directed to The Band who, Ella realised, had been humming softly to themselves since they'd left the bridge.

They stopped now.

'We did not sing.'

Bellboy didn't challenge them.

'My mistake. Having you here, it must be bringing back memories of the old days.'

'Speaking of which,' said Ella. 'This is probably as good a time as any to clear up what, precisely, is going on. So far, I've worked out that there was a Circus, some bad stuff went down and you're planning to nip back in time and put it right.'

'Not a bad summary,' admitted Bellboy. He paused, considering his next words carefully.

'The Psychic Circus was once a wonderful thing. A place where those of us who didn't fit in could... not fit in together. But it was corrupted. Taken over. It happened so slowly that many of us didn't realise until it was too late. The damage was already done.'

The Band nodded sadly.

'We were all changed.'

'And you,' Ella felt odd even saying it, as though it was somehow insensitive, 'died?'

Bellboy grinned.

'I did. Apparently.'

'You look good on it.'

'But also, I didn't. Obviously.'

'That's a great story. Have you thought about adapting it into a holo-novel?'

'Sorry. I know it's all very confusing. I wish I could explain more clearly but, to be honest, it's all a bit fuzzy. I was with the Circus, on a planet called Segonax. My... friend and I were trying to escape. Things had gone badly wrong somehow, I think. Then we got separated and... I stumbled across a ship. A broken ship.'

'The Vanguard.'

'Yes. They'd hit an eddy in the timestream and crash-landed. Decades before their own time and light years from home. We rescued each other. I was a mechanic. I promised to help fix their ship if they helped me find my friend and get us both off-world.'

Bellboy's voice slowed, and his eyes grew unfocused. It was apparently an effort to remember.

'Something went wrong,' prompted The Band.

'Yes. Or right, depending on how you look at it. As soon as I got the engines back online, the Vanguard time-jumped. Far into the future. At first, I was distraught. I'd left so many people behind. But then I realised the gift I'd been given. None of it had to happen in the first place. Gren took a little convincing, but underneath that gruff exterior...'

'Is a gruff interior?'

Bellboy laughed.

'Well, yes. But they've also lived a hell of a life. They knows what regret is. Since then, we've been travelling up and down the timestream, charting the Circus' course, narrowing down the moments at which its history is most vulnerable. And trying to recruit help, of course.'

'Unsuccessfully,' The Band noted.

'For the most part. Before you two, only Delios seemed to fully grasp what we were offering.'

'He was from the Circus too?' asked Ella. She wouldn't have said anything was beginning to make sense, as such, but the nonsense was beginning to take on a shape, which was something.

'Delios was once a struggling poet, from a planet of poets. Until the Circus came to his world. He thought he'd found somewhere he could stand out, but the Gods of Ragnarok, the power that had infected the Circus, decided it would be amusing to see what happened if they flooded his mind with all the words.' Bellboy's voice hardened with anger. 'And I mean *all* the words. At once.'

'That's terrible.'

'Our fate was similar,' added The Band. 'The Gods believed our harmonies to be imperfect. That the separation between our beings stood in our way.'

'So, these Gods, then. Sociopaths?'

'I've never met a God that wasn't.'

'And the plan is to go back and stop them.'

'Yes. Eventually. But first we have to get their attention.'

'And how do we do that?'

'We put on a show.'

*

When Ella came to, three or so minutes later, she had questions.

'Did I just sing?' being the first.

'Yes.'

'What the hell?'

'It was unexpected,' agreed The Band.

'What the actual hell?'

It came back to her slowly. They'd been talking. Bellboy had been explaining about the Gods of Ragnarok. And then there had been music. And it hadn't been like at Encore Station. There were no audio-bots, there was no stage. The music wasn't coming over the ship's comms. It was just *there*.

And unlike in her dreams, she *knew* the words. Knew exactly what to sing. Unsurprising, really, as she had sung about her life, about her childhood, about her hopes and fears.

About her parents.

About the mining colony.

And one other thing...

'Was it a duet?'

Bellboy nodded. He didn't seem perturbed in the slightest by the fact that they had just sung together for no apparent reason.

'Okay, that's it. That's my limit. Dodgy circuses and time travel and Gods, fine. But this is too much. How the hell did I know that song? And, more to the point, how did it know me?'

'We had to find a way to fight the Circus on its own terms,' explained Bellboy in a casual tone, as though talking them through the process of boiling water. Or breathing in and out. 'The Gods of Ragnarok want entertainment. They feed on it. So we're setting ourselves up in competition. Draw their victims away from the Circus in the past, undo the harm they've done.'

'That doesn't explain why I'm suddenly living in a musical.'

'Like I said, you'd be surprised at the tech that's available for the right price.'

'Nope. Do better.'

'The Vanguard is equipped with a low level psychic stimulation field. A *portable* psychic stimulation field.'

Ella stared at him hard.

'They're quite common for performers in the 31st century, I assure you. The field senses your emotions and helps you better translate them into music. Raises your game. Damps down your inhibitions. It's probably why the Band were humming the way they were.'

'You should have told us.' The Band's voices were stern. 'Music is a sacred thing.'

'I'm sorry. I'm so used to it now. I genuinely didn't think...'

'What's the point?'

'What do you mean?'

Ella stepped up to Bellboy and punctuated her words with a finger to his chest.

'What is the point of any of this?'

Bellboy took hold of her hand and gently lowered it, before rubbing the area of impact ruefully.

'It'll put us all on a level playing field when we come up against the Gods. Give them a show they'll remember.'

Ella was still furious. Or embarrassed. She couldn't quite make up her mind.

'And then?' she demanded.

'Oh, and then we kill them.'

*

When he returned to the bridge, sometime later, Bellboy was in a thoughtful mood. Thankfully, his arrival appeared to have coincided with a cessation of hostilities between the Captain and AJ.

The former was lounging in their command chair with their eyes firmly shut, although the lack of snoring[10] suggested they were still awake. The latter was chirruping their way through what Bellboy assumed to be the ordinary set of tasks for a patch of sentient rust in charge of navigating a starship.

Gren opened one eye at the sound of Bellboy's entrance.

'All settled in?' they asked.

'Yes.'

'Good.'

'Where's Delios?'

Gren grunted.

'I sent him to his room. For his own safety.'

Bellboy sighed for fear of laughing.

The Captain of the Vanguard opened the other eye and swivelled to face him. There was clearly something on their mind, a location that functioned better as a pit stop than somewhere to settle down.

'How did Ella take it?'

Case in point.

---

10. It is difficult to accurately conjure the snore of someone whose nose is constructed primarily from bark, but it is precisely as loud and as resonant as you'd imagine.

'How did she take what?'

Gren rolled their eyes.

'When you told her why she's most likely here.'

'I don't know why she's here.'

AJ's sunshine tones floated across the bridge.

'Bellboy, she looks just like her.'

This was a fact that Bellboy had been trying to dodge since he'd first laid eyes on Ella. Regardless of the surface differences, the longer he spent with her, the more the resemblance grew. She wasn't Flowerchild but, somehow, she was. The ramifications of that were unclear, so he had been relying on that much maligned problem-solving device known as denial.

'She looks a *bit* like her. And, most importantly, she is not her.'

Gren stood, their lack of stature utterly failing to affect their authority.

'I know that. But, come on. We've been all over time, twice, looking for this Flowerchild of yours.'

'I know.'

'And what have we found?'

'Gren...'

'Nothing. Nothing is what we've found. Every trace gone. As if she never existed.'

'She existed,' said Bellboy firmly.

'I'm not denying that.'

'Then what are you saying?'

'I'm saying that despite the clues we've left for her...'

'The messages,' added AJ, 'the invitations...

'That statue we erected to her on Janus II...'

'The symphonic suite you had composed in her honour and broadcast across the frontier world network...'

Bellboy sat down wearily on the stairs next to the command chair.

'I take your point.'

'Not even a blip, Bellboy. If she's out there, she's not answering.'

'Or can't.'

'Or can't, I grant you. On the other hand, we've been weirdly blasé about the fact that, just when we've almost exhausted our stack of very bad ideas, a young woman has appeared out of nowhere, looking *just like her* and claiming she doesn't know why she's here.'

'She's an orphan. Grew up on a mining colony.'

'She told you that?' asked AJ.

'She... sang it.'

'Oh well,' said Gren with mock sincerity, 'if she *sang* it.'

'You know how the field works. It's either the truth or she believes it to be the truth.'

'Those are not even close to being the same thing. As you know better than most.'

'I haven't given up on finding Flowerchild. The actual Flowerchild.'

'Nor should you,' said AJ, in a tone that implied a comforting hand to the shoulder.

'Don't encourage him,' snapped Gren. 'It's like trying to find a needle in... *all of space and time.*'

'We're getting closer. I can feel it.'

'Ah, but did you sing it?'

Bellboy stood, as if bolstered by the Captain's doubt.

'We've tested the waters for long enough. We need to make a proper start.'

'And what might a proper start entail?'

'Once we start making bigger adjustments to the timeline, hopefully things will get clearer.'

'That's what I thought you were going to say,' grumbled Gren. 'Although I held out a small hope you were going to suggest lunch.'

'There'll be time for lunch when the day's work is done.'

'That's really not how lunch works.'

Still, they straightened in their chair without further complaint and began to flip switches and punch buttons. Lights flickered across the navigator's console.

'Curtains up?' asked AJ.

'Curtains up,' confirmed Bellboy.

*

Ella settled into her bunk.

Or, more accurately, she lay on her bunk and squirmed, which was probably the best case scenario. The Vanguard was an amazing ship, there was no doubt about that, but it would never make it as a luxury cruiser. The room to which she had been assigned was wider than its single, barely padded bed, but only by the span of something particle physicists might get oddly excited about. The length was somewhat more accommodating, allowing room for a built-in

48

desk at the far end and a chair in which Ella would be tempted to sleep instead were it not constructed entirely of sharp edges.

It was, she reflected, the nicest room she'd ever had. The mining colony in which she had grown up went in for dormitory-style sleeping quarters. As a child, she had shared her living space with a dozen other girls of her age, all far too weary from their daily work to engage in anything approaching bonding. She had been lonely in a crowd.

She drew the communicator from her pocket and twisted its dial counterclockwise until it glowed a soft blue.

'Recording...' said a soft, artificial voice.

'Hi Mum,' said Ella, eyes fixed on the dull grey of the bulkhead above her. 'Ella here. Off on one of her crazy adventures again.'

She closed her eyes and let the words flow out of her.

'You know how you used to say, when I was little, that the universe was there to be explored and I should never be afraid to step out into it?'

She let out a near silent, self-directed laugh.

'Of course you don't. Because you never said it. Well, maybe you did, but not to me. Too busy being dead, I suppose. It does seem like a bit of a time sink.'

Ella cricked her neck and turned onto her side.

'Speaking of... I'm about to travel to the past and fight some Old Gods with showtunes, so I'll probably be seeing you soon.'

Loneliness, Ella imagined, was a universal constant. There were too many people around for it not to be. But she knew, deep down, that she had been isolated for so long that she rarely felt it consciously.

She felt it now.

'Goodnight,' she whispered into the recorder, before powering it down. 'Love to Dad.'

'Recording terminated,' offered the device by way of commiseration.

Ella closed her eyes. Sleep would be a fine thing. Sure, everything would likely still be insane in the morning, but she'd have more energy to deal with it.

She had almost dropped off when she was disturbed by the telltale first chords of a rousing ensemble ballad.

She sat up, quite against her will. Felt a verse spill into her mind.

'What fresh hell is this?' she managed before she began to sing.

*

Further down the corridor, Delios sat scribbling at his desk, an old-fashioned quill scratching lines into an even more old-fashioned sheet of genuine, non-replicated paper.

Before the Gods had destroyed his mind, he had been a mediocre poet, with moments of inspiration. Now that his work made absolutely no sense, it was possible he might be taken for a genius.

For him, however, it was torture, pure and simple. All of those words, across hundreds of languages, lodged in his head and begging to be released. And all of them in dispute with their neighbours, unwilling or unable to cooperate, to unite, to form something greater than themselves.

But still, he wrote. He could do nothing else. In what few entirely lucid moments he had, he knew that, for the first time in his life, he had something unique and powerful to say. If only he had been left the means to express it.

When the music began for him, leaping down the corridor from Ella's verse to Delios' impassioned chorus, he felt a mixture of relief and despair wash over him.

He would sing a fraction of how he felt.

It wasn't enough.

But it was something.

*

Bellboy was on his way to his own cabin when the song struck him. He had grown accustomed to singing at random intervals, had almost begun to enjoy it. Like Ella, he had felt alone often. Before Flowerchild and after Flowerchild: the shapes of solitude.

Like Delios, he often struggled to express his finer feelings. He thought some of his friends might find that idea amusing; he could be verbose, almost theatrical. But the depths. The core. The heart. These things existed in hints and teases only.

Except when the field struck and he sang. The man who was Bellboy revealed at last. For better or for worse.

Together apart, the three travellers sang.

*

The Band of Infinite Harmony sat on the edge of their bunk, in the dark of their cabin, seemingly immune to the song ranging through the ship.

They were not silent, however.

The Band hummed. The same snatch of tune that had escaped their lips earlier. Over and over. At times, barely more than a vibration of their lips. At others, a groaning, heartbreaking sound.

Was it done unconsciously? A side effect of the psychic stimulation field? A memory fragmented through four consciousnesses?

If they knew, they were not telling.

Chapter Five

The Vanguard was in orbit around Delios' homeworld of Othrys. This had caused, perhaps unsurprisingly at this juncture, an argument.

'Ding!' AJ had proclaimed, matter-of-factly.

'I'm sorry,' Captain Gren had replied. 'Did you just say *ding*?'

'Yes.'

'I'm afraid to ask, but why?'

AJ cleared her throat and quoted from the Vanguard's operations manual. A book that did not exist outside of the navigator's mind but to which she referred often.

'On arrival, the ship's systems are programmed to emit a commanding, sonorous, bell-like sound to alert all passengers and crew to our arrival at any given destination.'

'And?' Gren did not like any of the potential answers to this question but they were in too deep now.

'It broke.'

'How?'

'I'd rather not say.'

'You'd rather say ding?"

'It got your attention, didn't it?' In fact, the ship's orbit alarm had been damaged when AJ had attempted to add a subroutine to its trigger system that would enable it to adjust its key to whatever song was currently doing the rounds of the ship. This seemed a reasonable and potentially satisfying task to her, but it was not an explanation she deemed likely to ease the Captain's obvious frustration.

'Yes, but you just randomly said *ding*. I had no idea what it was for. Supper might have been ready.'

The supper alarm is a clear quarter tone higher, thought AJ, though she wisely kept this observation to herself.

'You have a viewscreen?' she chirruped instead.

Gren groaned. They had a feeling they knew where this was going.

'Yes.'

'You can see the frankly enormous planet?'

They had no problem with evolution producing a patch of rust that could think, speak and feel, but a cheeky one felt an advancement too far.

'Yes.'

'And the navigation system has shifted into orbital approach.'

'It has.'

'I thought you'd put two and two together.'

Gren leant back in their chair, a riposte finally occurring.

'Yes, well,' they said, 'we'll just have to see how well our *passengers* fared without the benefit of context clues.'

The door behind them opened; Bellboy strode onto the bridge, Delios tucked into his wake.

'I heard a ding,' said Bellboy. 'I assume we've reached Othrys.'

'Thanks for nothing,' said Captain Gren.

'If it were a bell that rung,' Delios added, 'A parting precedes acts unsung.'

'Took the words out of my mouth.' Bellboy touched Delios' hand lightly. 'So, my friend. There is it. Home. How do you feel?"

'For the love of all that is transportable,' cautioned Gren, 'don't ask him how he feels. We'll never make planetfall.'

The door slid back again, this time admitting Ella and The Band.

Before either could open their mouths, Gren cut in.

'Yes, there was a ding,' they said, with an air of weary resignation. 'Yes, it means we've arrived.'

'I figured. *Where* have we arrived?"

'Our first professional engagement,' said Bellboy pointedly. Then he turned to The Band. 'You weren't with us at Othrys, were you? The first time, I mean.'

'We did not have that pleasure.'

'Othrys is a planet of poetry. Not pleasure.'

'So,' said Ella gingerly, 'this is where Delios...'

'Yes.'

AJ piped up from her station.

'Captain, we're receiving a private transmission from the surface.'

'You don't have a noise for that?' asked Gren.

'Now you're just being silly.'

'Put it through.'

There was a brief burst of subspace static that soon resolved into a voice. It was the sort of voice that made you want to search for sea monsters or blow into a bag made from skin. No one quite understood why.

It was also, quite clearly, the voice of a practiced performer.

'The sky is blue,' it intoned. 'And so is the sea. Welcome to Othrys. It... erm... welcomes thee.'

Practice, it seemed, did not always make perfect.

'Is that it?' asked Gren.

'That was the end of the transmission,' confirmed AJ.

Bellboy looked to Delios.

'Who was that?'

The poet seemed almost embarrassed.

'A man apart. A part of a man.'

There was a tinkle of light and sound from AJ's station as she consulted the computer.

'I believe that was the High Poet of Othrys. The planet's spiritual and cultural leader.'

'That's new. I don't remember meeting him the last time. Also, isn't the sky orange on Othrys?'

'And the sea it burns,' added Delios with surprising clarity, 'a colour unspeakable.'

'Poetic licence?'

Another series of bleeps from the memory banks.

'According to my records, he is a strict traditionalist on the rhyming front. And, you know, *orange*...'

If a sentient patch of rush *could* give a knowing look, AJ would have. She had a damned good try regardless.

56

'I'm starting to feel nostalgic for the golden days of *ding*,' offered Gren.

Bellboy clapped his hands together. He seemed almost gleeful, which didn't suit him one bit.

'Right. Let's see if we can arrange ourselves a landing bay. Business beckons.'

*

Othrys.

The Planet of Poets. The World of Wordsmiths. The Sphere of Sonnets. These were just some of the names the Tourist Information Guild had tried to convince their galactic neighbours to put into circulation, but to no avail.[11]

The sentence actually used by most outsiders, when referring to Othrys was:

'I mean, it's all right as a hobby, I suppose.'

This was usually said loudly in the presence of any offspring that appeared suspiciously bookish.

The intolerant mainstream was one thing, however, with their love of eating every day and changing their socks more often than biannually.

Those in the know – the cultured – still came to Othrys in droves. To hear poetry, write poetry, take part in the historically bloody and therefore marketable Poetry Crucibles and generally just swan about feeling superior to anyone who didn't 'get it'.

You might imagine that a planet made up entirely of bards, rather than, say, engineers or city planners

---

11. As everyone knows, you can't choose your own nickname. It must be bestowed upon you. And when it is, you will not care for it.

might suffer when it came to infrastructure. Your average artiste, stereotypically, might describe in detail how plumbing had impacted their worldview but they couldn't always lay hands on a plunger. But these were poets who had worked out a way to consistently monetise their art and therefore were not to be underestimated. Besides, visitors needed something to wax poetically about and they couldn't guarantee – their lawyers maintained – tragic romances or startling new insights into parental relationships.

For that they needed inspiring vistas, overpriced poetry-themed attractions and bars, lots of bars, so that romantic entanglements and realisations about Mother's private life remained attainable in theory.

They did their best to keep it on brand. In this, the capital city of Othrys, known only as The Page, you might plan a meditative walk along the Iambic Perimeter, take in the glistening majesty of Cadence Falls or, if you were feeling saucy, squire a companion to an Enjambment Jamboree.[12]

Bellboy and his crew were currently making their way down Lyric Avenue, a mile-long thoroughfare that led from the landing pads at Diphthong Bay to the great Assonance Crossroads. It was lined with stalls selling everything from quill nibs to holo-photos

---

12. Needless to say, Othrys' commercial sectors were a nightmare to the pun averse. The most successful franchise in the planet's history – to give you some idea – was a chain of open mic emporiums called *Stanza and Deliver*. That this horrific play on words worked – or failed to work, depending on your sensitivities – regardless of the translation matrix through which it was processed – is an oddly under-researched phenomenon.

58

of Othrys' most famous versifiers, at prices inflated to suit the ignorance of the outsider.

The owners had all taken great pains to appear as authentic and unshowy as possible, favouring, as they announced their wares, an earthy patois that in no way reflected the way they spoke around their family's estate.

The number of couplet enhancers available for a single Othrysian alcaic[13] was a subject much discussed.

'It's exactly how I remember it,' mused Bellboy. 'Not that we saw much of the city back then. The Circus kept us busy.'

'You performed here?' asked Ella. She wouldn't have enjoyed admitting it, but the sheer scale of what she was seeing had left her feeling overwhelmed. When she was a child, she saw her quarters and the mine. That was it. Since then, she'd seen a selection of identical cargo holds, Encore Station and the Vanguard. To have set foot on an entirely new world was exciting but it was also terrifying. She hoped that if she kept asking questions it would allow her brain enough of a head-start to understand some of the answers.

'Flowerchild and I were the newbies then,' Bellboy explained, with a touch of melancholy. 'The Circus was not yet... what it became.'

---

13. The Othrysian monetary system was elegant, if potentially confusing to the neophyte. There were, in the simplest terms, ten alcaics to each allegoric, but their actual worth shifted moment-to-moment based on the relative life satisfaction of the bearer. A happy person was deemed to need less and, therefore, their cash was devalued. The ability to scowl convincingly was key to any successful transaction on Othrys.

'The darkness was waiting,' muttered Delios. 'Shifting, shy and sullen. Already hungry, feeding on scraps. A shadow waiting on a sun.'

'So true, my friend.'

Ella turned to The Band. They hadn't said much since their arrival on Othrys, content, it appeared, to hang back and take it all in. Ella assumed that someone with four faces could observe like nobody's business.

'What about you?' she asked.

'We had not yet encountered the Circus. We were not yet one.'

'Always one,' said Delios, a note of pain creeping into his voice. 'And then one more Two plus two. And three and four.' The poet had been more than usually distracted since they'd hit orbit. Which was understandable; this was where – and when – his life had changed forever.

Bellboy stopped and addressed them all.

'My friends, I know this is difficult. We're in the lion's den now.'

There was something at the edge of his words that suggested he was talking as much to himself as anyone. Despite all it had taken to get here, this was the first time his theories – his plan – would really be tested.

'You've trusted me this far,' he offered.

'Have we?' asked Ella. Her own nerves were starting to get the better of her.

'You're here, aren't you? And *here* is where I finally prove that the future is written not in stone, but in ever drifting sands.'

The impact of his proclamation was slightly diluted by the mechanical hum that followed it and the sudden, unexpected appearance of a shimmering male figure.

'Sand, hmm?' it said. 'Let's see. Some sand in the hand saves the beast from the brand.'

It was the voice they had heard on the ship – that of the High Poet – and it was attached to a short man with closely cropped hair and an air of perpetual bemusement. His flowing robes were similar to those Delios wore, albeit with fewer loose threads around the cuffs and without the faint aroma of having been slept in for a week.

Bellboy held up a calming, authoritative hand.

'Stay calm, everyone. It's just a hologram.'

Ella was relieved to hear this confirmed, as it explained neatly why the High Poet was currently semi-transparent and hovering.

It would have felt rude to enquire directly.

The High Poet nodded solemnly.

'A hologram for sir. For ma'am. Visitors to our fair land.'

His face crumpled into a frown.

'Land? No, not land. That hard 'D' spoils the whole thing.' He chewed his lip in thought for a moment, then shook his head. 'I'll begin again. A hologram for sir. For ma'am...' He trailed off, the requisite resolution refusing to form.

'A wolf that feeds not on the lamb.'

The High Poet grinned and turned to Delios, who was now focusing with great intent on his own sandals.

'Oh, that's very good. *A wolf that feeds not on the lamb.* Yes. Powerful but with a hidden gentility. I'll steal that if you don't mind.'

Delio did not reply. Or look up. He seemed to still be breathing, but Ella wouldn't have minded the opportunity to check for certain.

The High Poet floated gently towards him, holographic eyes roaming up and down the beleaguered wordsmith.

'But, of course, I should have expected nothing less, I see you bear the mark of our order. A poet, though I was not immediately aware of the fact.'

Ella leaned towards The Band.

'Is that *good* poetry?' she whispered. 'I don't have much experience to draw on.'

'It is not.'

'That's a relief. I was beginning to wonder what all the fuss was about.'

'It may, however, be avant-garde,' added The Band.

'Avant-garde is far too hard,' the High Poet chimed in, seemingly oblivious to the previous criticism. 'A well-matched couplet is my...'

His voice died away once more and he squinted into the middle distance for an uncomfortably long period before finally shrugging.

'Well, it's usually mine, at any rate.'

The High Poet of Othrys flicked a mote of holographic dust from his shoulder and stared at them each in turn. He seemed to be waiting for something. Possibly applause.

None was forthcoming.

'But I'm drifting off-track,' he said, managing to look only mildly disgruntled. 'Allow me to introduce myself. I am the High Poet of Othrys. And you are?'

Bellboy seized his moment.

'We are the Songs of the Unsung,' he announced with gusto.

Ella and The Band exchanged glances. We're *who*?

'A travelling troupe of musicians and singers,' Bellboy continued. 'We're hoping to arrange a performance.'

The High Poet considered this.

'Hmm,' he said. 'Tunes are cheating, of course, but...' His voice took on a new warmth. 'Othrys welcomes devotees of all the Muses. If music be the food of love, as a Terran of my acquaintance once remarked... let's do lunch.'

Bellboy inclined his head.

'It would be an honour.'

The High Poet fumbled at the sleeves of his robe and there was a series of electronic beeps.

'Directions have been uploaded to your navigation device. I shall expect you within the hour.'

There was a fizz and a faint pop as the hologram disappeared.

'I don't like him,' said Ella.

'At the height of all, depths are drowned.'

'You are too gracious for your own good, Delios,' said Bellboy.

The hologram reappeared as quickly as it had vanished, causing Ella to yelp.

'My apologies,' said the High Poet. 'Just one final question. You do have hours where you come from, yes? I always forget to ask.'

'Far too many,' said The Band.

'That's funny,' mused the High Poet, 'I've always found the opposite.'

63

'We're fully set to local time,' Bellboy assured him.

'An hour then. An hour ten.'

The High Poet gave his audience one last appraising look, as if preparing to leave them with a final pearl of wisdom. Possibly even an entire oyster.

'Depending on traffic,' he said.

And then he was gone again.

Bellboy looked thoughtful for a moment, then gathered his troops.

'Right,' he said. 'This is where we divide and conquer. Delios, you and I have, it would appear, a royal appointment to prepare for.'

'What about us?' asked Ella.

'I have another task in mind for you.'

*

It is a truth universally[14] acknowledged, that an artist, having achieved any degree of financial success, will inevitably end up living in a ridiculous house.

The High Poet of Othrys was no exception. Like all Othrysian citizens, he had begun life in penury,[15] before gradually, by the sweat of his pen, working his way up to his current exalted status.

That he done so without any perceptible talent was not considered unusual, far less an insult to the

---

14. And we don't the use term lightly.

15. Othrysian children, regardless of the success of their parents, were sent to live in large, draughty, orphanage-like buildings from a formative age, as a way of building literary character. And, it has to be said, to prevent them from writing epic pastiches about how difficult it is to find a decent pony groom these days.

craft. On a planet where everyone was an artist, it was argued, a High Poet must be all things to all people. If he were too good, too accomplished or unique, he would cease to be an aspirational figure. In plain terms, the emotion his role was intended to engender was, 'I can do better than *that.*'

On those grounds, he was the most successful High Poet to ever hold the office.

He also, better than most, knew how to manage optics. The Abode of the High Poet, as his traditional accommodations were known, had been commissioned centuries before, but he had truly made them his own.

For instance, they had always been, by design, in appalling taste, but only the current High Poet had fully seen their potential to be eye-wateringly, obscenely *wrong.*

The outer structure was made entirely of artificially distressed marble, which was bad enough. And then there were the pillars. So *many* pillars. Most of which clearly weren't holding up anything at all. They were just hanging around, like a group of youths in a parking lot.

Inside, however, was where things truly became vomit-worthy. On every wall, in every room, hung a painting of the High Poet himself, posed as if about to deliver his most famous work, *Ode to an Insultingly Inconsequential Royalty Payment.* The pictures were a gift from the artists on Hathrys, Othrys' sister world, and ranged in style from grotesque charcoal drawings to grotesque watercolours.

He was, of course, nude and lightly oiled in all of them.

Where there had been deemed insufficient wall space in a room, a similarly disturbing sculpture or holographic projection took their place.

The entrance hall, where Bellboy and Delios awaited their official audience with the High Poet, was, mercifully, the only place in the house not thus adorned. Alas, its walls were instead lined with framed squares of cloth on which some unfortunate had been forced to needlepoint quotes from classic[16] poems.

As Delios shuffled uncomfortably behind him, Bellboy was staring down a noxious concoction describing the proximity between love and laughter. He felt the sharp tang of bile rising in his throat.

'The past, it bites,' Delios exclaimed suddenly. 'It tears and gnaws. Unfurls its wings, unsheathes its claws.'

Bellboy hurried over to him.

'What is it?'

'Hunger paces, craves its place at the table.'

Delios grabbed Bellboy's hand and pulled it to his chest, hard. It was so uncharacteristically tactile that Bellboy almost recoiled. Instead, he leaned in, placing his forehead to that of his troubled friend.

'I'm sorry this is so difficult for you. But we're going to fix things. I swear it.'

'An oath is served, so cool and crisp. But an oath is simply a fool with a lisp.'

Bellboy leaned back and stared into the seemingly guileless face in front of him.

---

16. An Othrysian word meaning 'without specific artistic value but oddly ubiquitous.'

'Was that a joke?'

But Delios wasn't laughing. However near to love it was. If anything, he was breaking through.

'Please,' he said, all haziness dropping from his voice. 'I don't want to.'

Bellboy's eyes widened. Somehow, he knew that had been the real Delios, the one that existed before the Circus took a turn around his mind. Was that a good or a bad thing? Did it mean they were having an effect?

Or, less reassuringly, that the Gods were making a pre-emptive strike?

Before he could explore further, the High Poet swept into the hall. In the flesh, this time. Although, happily for all concerned, in less of the flesh than in his portraits.

'Greetings, my friends. I'm sorry there was no one to meet you. It's not considered seemly for a poet to have servants. Frankly, it's a miracle they allow me to bathe.'

This was not strictly true. Yes, the employment of domestic staff was considered improper for an artist. However, they were expected to allow childhood friends, aspiring disciples and other general hangers-on to see to the day-to-day running of things, in exchange for a little reflected glory.

But the High Poet had no entourage. Whether this was because he had been an unpopular child or had become too imposing a figure on the cultural scene or simply because he had decorated his entire home with nude paintings of himself, no one could say with complete certainty.

It was probably the paintings though.

'High Poet,' began Bellboy

'Please. Call me Ishmael.'

'Ishmael?'

'Oh, it's not my name. I simply heard it somewhere and I always thought it sounded like tremendous fun.' He closed his eyes and intoned the word like a mantra. 'Ishmael.'

Delios seemed less convinced.

'Nameless, nameless, nameless dread. Infects the heart, inflames the head.'

The High Poet's eyes snapped open.

'Very well. High Poet then. It makes little difference to me. And please, there's no need to versify here. We're off the clock.'

'I'm afraid my friend here is never off the clock.'

The High Poet nodded.

'I understand. I was the same when I was a young poet. Forever trying to make my mark. Impress the muckity-mucks with my verbal acuity. Eventually, they made me High Poet, so I suppose there's something in it.'

He tried to catch Delios' eye and failed. 'You verse away, lad. One day, all this could be yours.'

'With every word I fail to use, my sentence is completed.'

'I see. A modernist.' The High Poet wrinkled his nose. 'Never mind. We all go through that phase.' He turned back to Bellboy. 'Now, I understand that you want to arrange a performance of some kind. A musical *extravaganza*.'

'That's right. Is it possible?'

'Everything is *possible*. So, yes. But better still, it's plausible. We happen, I've been informed, to have had a cancellation at the Great Arena. A company of free verse advocates were booked to perform, but they had a falling out over the use of punctuation – or lack thereof.' He rolled his eyes heavenwards. 'It happens more often than you'd think. Could you be ready by tomorrow?'

'More than.'

'More than ready? I'll be curious to see what that looks like. I'd have though it meant you'd already finished. But excellent. Speak to Gregoria at the Arena, they'll look after you.'

Bellboy smiled. He was doing his best to appear grateful while fighting off a deep sense of this having all gone too smoothly.

'Thank you, High Poet.'

'My pleasure,' the elder scribe replied, in a half-hearted tone that stripped all meaning from the word. 'You're fortunate to have come when you did. We've been inundated with off-world proposals of late. There's even a Circus due in town next month. Something to do with cyclists if you can believe it. Young people do have some funny ideas.'

The hair on the back of Bellboy's neck stood to attention, clearly misled by the military cut of his jacket.

'We'll do our best not to let you down,' he said evenly.

The High Poet made as if to leave.

'Good. We have high standards on Othrys. Isn't that right, Delios?'

The younger poet looked up, startled, to find the High Poet's eyes locked on his.

'He knows my aspect. Knows my voice.'

Something had shifted in the High Poet's demeanour. It wasn't that he'd become sinister as such. There was no abrupt burst of cackling. But a single layer of wooliness had sloughed away, revealing a glimpse of the man capable of rising to the most powerful post on his world.

'I know all my poets. And, ordinarily, I'd look askance at them falling in with musicians. But I'm just happy to discover you're doing something. I'd received some worrying reports to the contrary.'

He let the final sentence linger, lending particular attention to the r's.

'We won't take up any more of your time, High Poet,' said Bellboy.

The High Poet held Delios in his gaze a little longer, like a rattlesnake reluctant to pardon a mouse. Then, as if a switch had been flipped, all was once again the height of chummy bonhomie.

'No, I don't suppose you will. Farewell, singers – to your songs. Let's meet again before ere long.' He gifted his visitors a theatrical wink. 'Professional tip – always throw in an 'ere' or two. It classes things up.'

*

'This is completely humiliating.'

'It is a necessary evil.'

'Ah,' said Ella, 'so you admit it's evil.'

She was standing in the heart of the Promotional District, where performers went to advertise their

70

shows to the potential audiences. To prevent complete deforestation of the planet, printed materials were strictly prohibited. Each act or group was given access to an electronic billboard, about four feet in width, and assigned to one of a series of raised dais that ran down the centre of the street. What they did after that was up to them.

The Band had, to their credit and Ella's surprise, proved extremely adept at condensing the essence of their, until earlier, entirely imaginary show into a vague but eye-catching series of images that now slid across the billboard screen at thirty second intervals. But they still had to do the heavy lifting.

'The Songs of the Unsung,' The Band told the passing crowds, 'have come to Othrys. Music to soothe the most savage breast. The ballads of a thousand worlds.'

Ella tended to think of The Band's voice as a monotone which was inherently inaccurate. It was flat, however. She supposed it was difficult to express nuance through four competing sets of vocal chords. In some strange way, they cancelled each other out. It did not, in any case, make them the most compelling choice for spokespeople.

She was fairly certain that if it weren't for the relentless flow of the foot traffic, they'd be putting passers-by to sleep.

Frustrated with her own reluctance, she ground her teeth. Get it together, Ella, she thought. This was important. Show willing. Be part of the team.

She took a deep breath.

'The galaxy's greatest melodies!' she bellowed.

The communicator in her pocket bleeped. It was perhaps the happiest sound she'd ever heard. She drew out the device eagerly and twisted its dial.

'Ella,' came Bellboy's voice, skipping over the niceties, 'You need to go to the Arena and speak to someone called Gregoria.'

'Sure,' said Ella. The Arena sounded like somewhere that was not here. She was all in favour. 'Why?'

'To negotiate fees.'

'Got it.'

'Fees?' asked The Band, listening in.

'We have,' said Bellboy, 'a gig.'

*

Bellboy strode onto the bridge of the Vanguard while, behind him, quite incapable of anything as forceful as striding, Delios consistently failed to stop moving.

Gren's command chair swivelled to face them. Gren, being in it, went along for the ride.

'We're on,' Bellboy announced.

'When?'

'When the moon holds its infant in its arms,' said Delios, 'and makes its silent promise.'

'Tomorrow?!'

'Yes, AJ. Tomorrow.'

Gren scratched their chin. They were less perturbed by the acceleration of events than Bellboy had feared. But they still, inevitably, had thoughts.

'It's not impossible, but it's tight. We need to get the stimulation field in place. We need to check out

72

the acoustics. We need to make sure we're not getting done over on the box office.'

'It's all under control, Captain.' Bellboy smiled. 'I have my best people on it.'

*

The Great Arena at Othrys is not to be found on any list of any of the hundreds of places and sights referred to colloquially as the Wonders of the Universe. And not because it doesn't deserve to be. It has grandeur. It has elegance. It has a long, rich history about which many boring books have been written. By any rights, on a day when the sun hit its sleek curves just right, it might even be in with a chance of the top slot, should such a thing ever be agreed upon.

So why is it excluded?

For one simple reason. It's too successful.

Other Wonders may be more popular tourist attractions. Some were certainly more visually stunning. More naturally astonishing. They may have had an incalculable impact on the growth and development of civilisations or contain and preserve knowledge beyond imagining. Some of them may even make money.

But they are not the Great Arena at Othrys. That is something else again.

It is a going concern. And, as such, if it were even nominated, you'd be unlikely to get hold of anyone in authority for long enough to arrange a holo-shoot.

Ella knew none of this, which is the only reason she was able to knock on the enormous wooden gate at its entrance with anything like expectation.

It is also why she was not sufficiently surprised when it was opened almost immediately.

'Are you here about the drains?' asked the figure who appeared from behind it. She was dressed in poets' robes of a rich burgundy[17] and would clearly be handy in a fight.

Her name was Gregoria.

Gregoria to her friends and Gregoria to her enemies, some of whom were also her friends.

She was one of the most feared people on Othrys. Someone who could make or break careers. Who knew where the bodies were buried. Partially because, it was rumoured, she had been responsible for putting them there in the first place.

Gregoria worked Front of House for the Great Arena.

'We are not here about the drains,' answered The Band.

'We're from the Songs of the Unsung,' added Ella quickly, the look on the woman's face suggesting she had mislaid most of her patience before their arrival and couldn't swear to the quality of the remainder.

'Oh, I see,' said Gregoria, nodding. 'Well, that's fine then.' Then she began to close the gate.

Ella, in a classic case of it seemed like a good idea in the moment, lodged it open with her foot.

Gregoria looked at the gate. Then she looked at the foot. Then she looked at the owner of the foot and wordlessly demanded an explanation.

---

17. Unlike in some cultures, Othrysian robe colours told you little about the role or status of the wearer. Darker shades, however, were often chosen by those with a preference for sloppier foods.

'We're a travelling troupe of musicians and singers.'

'Sounds dreadful. What's it got to do with me?'

'The High Poet sent us,' said The Band.

Gregoria peered curiously at them. Then turned her attention to Ella, who she had clearly judged to be, if not the brains of the operation, then the least likely to occasion a felony.

'What's wrong with your friend's face?' she asked.

Ella was reaching the end of her own tether.

'Perhaps you should ask them yourself.'

The proposition was accepted.

'What's wrong with your face?'

'We are The Band of Infinite Harmony.'

'I thought you were the Songs of the Unstrung?'

'The Unsung.' If this was some sort of hazing ritual, Ella thought, then she and Bellboy would be singing a rather fiery call-and-response number when they returned to the ship.

'And them.'

Ella clenched and unclenched her fists.

'As my friend mentioned, the High Poet sent us. Apparently, you've a cancellation tomorrow and, well, we're the replacements.'

This didn't exactly mollify the gatekeeper but it did, usefully, redirect her ire.

'You know,' she said, 'I'm getting mighty fed up with His Holiness thinking he can send over whoever he likes, whenever he likes. This is the Great Arena. Not the backroom of a slam bar. I've a waiting list as long as a piece of annotated juvenilia back there.' She jerked a thumb over her shoulder. 'I don't need to take in acts off the street.'

'We assure you,' said The Band, 'we are aware of the storied history of this venue and what it represents to the people of this world.'

'Of course you are. Everyone is.'

'We'll work for a cut of the refreshments takings,' said Ella.

Gregoria opened the gate wide.

'Welcome to the Great Arena.'

*

'Put it through.'

'Yes, Captain.'

Ella's voice filled the Vanguard's bridge.

'We're on our way back.'

Bellboy stood next to Gren's command chair and tried to sound nonchalant. His nerves were beginning to jangle now, to the point that he feared they would soon form the backing to a throwaway number about conquering his fears.

He felt chalant. Almost entirely chalant.

'Everything sorted with the Arena?'

'Well, I'd keep the light show budget to a minimum, but it's all booked.'

'Good work, Ella. But before you come back here, I've got another little job for you.'

'Oh, good.'

*

One of the first things they tell you about time travel – one of the first things about which they *warn* you – is the potentially universe-ending risks of crossing timelines. *Verboten* is the word. Even in that universe where Germany is populated entirely by mimes.

You should certainly avoid, at all costs, meeting your younger self or making pals with your great-grandmother or arranging it so that you break up with an ex before they can break up with you.

What they don't tell you is that following these rules to the letter renders time travel all but useless.

'So is this an average day in the entertainment business?'

Ella and The Band were standing outside a small, untidy-looking house in one of the less salubrious residential regions. These were known as dues-paying districts, home to poets who had yet to make a name for themselves.

'How do you mean?'

'Shouting in the street, banging on doors, generally being treated like dirt?'

Ella had worked down a mine, forever dark and usually freezing, since she was three years old. Despite which, she was beginning to think that showfolk were masochists.

'Oh. Yes, this is much like other days we have known.'

'When this is all over, I might look into something in accounting.'

She knocked.

If a door can open desperately, this one did.

'Greetings,' said the young poet who stood before them. His robes were a little cleaner, his hair was thicker and his eyes were startlingly clear. But there was no mistaking him.

'I welcome you to the House of Delios. Would you care for a sonnet?'

'Maybe later,' said Ella and socked him in the jaw.

He went down like a sack of recently punched poet.

'Poetry,' The Band observed, 'is an especially difficult field.'

*

An hour later, on the Vanguard bridge, Bellboy decided it had been too long between inspirational speeches.

'I want to thank you all for your hard work today. I know that there is more at stake than any of us can properly express. So, I thank you for your trust. For your patience. And, as of tomorrow, for your voices.'

There was a smattering of reflexive applause to which AJ added a whistle of encouragement.

'What are we going to do with past Delios?' asked Ella. 'I feel a little bad. I mean, he'll probably get the beginnings of a ballad out of it, but, still. Sorry, by the way.'

This was addressed to the current Delios. His reaction to the sight of his younger self, as yet untouched by Gods, had been oddly muted. But even that, in its own way, was just another reminder of why they were doing this.

'An old pain, not yet felt. An old wound, not yet dealt.'

'I just hope you understand why I did it. When you're him, I mean. Hold on, will you be him? Or will he be you? I'm still working out this time travel stuff.'

'We all are, trust me,' said Bellboy. 'And Gren and AJ will look after Delios. We can't risk him showing up. If the Gods are watching – the longer they remain unaware of our true purpose, the better.'

'So we put him back when we're done.'

During the journey to Othrys, Ella had asked Bellboy to explain the plan to her in more detail. He had attempted to do so, at one point using an elaborate chart and a number of coloured stickers. It hadn't cleared much up but it was undeniably pretty.

'We put him back,' corrected Captain Gren, 'when we know we've changed the timeline.'

'In the original version of events,' said Bellboy, 'Delios performed or, rather, attempted to perform, an extremely challenging piece of free verse.'

'The poor devil,' muttered Gren.

'But he froze up on stage and was subsequently ostracised by the entire poetic community. He was ruined.'

'Then,' added The Band, 'the Circus came to town.'

Bellboy's voice darkened, as it always did when he recalled the Gods' machinations.

'They prey on the vulnerable.'

'So,' said Ella, 'we keep both versions of him offstage. Will that... fix him?'

'I hope so. That is the idea. One less victim for the Circus. One less *soldier* for the Circus.'

'And then?'

'With any luck, the Gods begin to wonder if perhaps they should look elsewhere for their entertainment. And before long, they're the ones who are vulnerable.'

'And torches in hand, they approached the pyre. Their duty set in stone.' A flicker of grim satisfaction passed over Delios' features.

'This is all beginning to feel very real,' said Ella, 'And, just so you know, that has not been the vibe up to this point.'

'I think everyone should take some time to prepare. In whatever manner works for them. Tomorrow, we go to war.'

All but the Captain and Bellboy made their way to the exit.

'Actually, Ella,' Bellboy called. 'I think you and I should take a little walk. There's something you should probably see.'

*

If you spend any amount of time travelling the universe, you will begin to pick up on certain patterns, things that crop up in multiple cultures in one form or another regardless of surface differences.

Love. Family. War. Foreheads of varying degrees of bumpiness.

Bars.

It would appear that whatever unifying force connects all lifeforms, throughout creation, it has decreed a primal need to gather together in set places and, more often than not, imbibe something fermented.

Bars on Othrys were, perhaps needless to say, poetry heavy. And drinks on Othrys were strong.[18] Any connection between the two is neither inferred nor untrue.

---

18. See the famous folk ballad *I Went to Othrys, Probably.*

Ella and Bellboy sat at a rickety wooden table as fragments of doggerel and limerick fluttered around them.

'You have an interesting definition for *walk*,' the young woman shouted against the noise.

She lifted her glass and stared at the thick purple liquid in it[19] before taking an exploratory sip. It wasn't bad.

It wasn't good either.

'Not that I'm complaining,' she added. 'It's nice to find a planet where I'm old enough to get served.

Bellboy stared into those almost familiar eyes.

'How old are you, exactly, Ella?'

'I think I'm about eighteen.'

'You think?'

She took another long swallow of her drink. It really was very nearly pleasant.

'The mining corporations aren't exactly sticklers for paperwork... orphan-wise.'

Bellboy leant back in his chair, as though retreating from the tragedy of the story.

'And you were just left with them?'

'That's what they told me. My parents were killed in an accident, the corporation took me on. When they decided I was of age, I was given a choice. Sign a contract or do for myself. I chose the latter.'

It was true. The corporation had a strange relationship with servitude. It was perfectly acceptable

---

19. Othrysian ale. A beverage with the unique property that it grows more potent on contact with humanoid digestive systems, meaning you don't get drunk until several hours after drinking it. Brewed, as their slogan explains, 'once by us and once by you.'

for the children in its charge to work fourteen hour days in unsafe conditions, but adult workers had to be there of their own volition. She suspected it was because very few children knew lawyers.

'Do you remember your parents at all?'

'Flashes? Maybe? For all I know, the people I picture when I think about my parents were some random miners. What about you?'

'Once you join the Circus, everything before gets a little... hazy.'

'No family then.'

'Oh, I didn't say that. There was someone.'

'Your *friend*.' Ella teased him.

'Her name was Flowerchild.' Like a crashing wave, the memory of her washed over him. Her face, her voice, her touch, her absence. 'I loved her very much.'

'I'm sorry. I didn't mean...'

Bellboy smiled. 'She didn't think I had much of a sense of humour either.'

Ella shook her head. She'd spent so long on her own that navigating other people's emotions felt like being down the mines again. Only she was wearing a hood. And was in a box.

'Well, surely, all this... everything we're doing... you're going to find her too? Save her?'

Before Bellboy could answer, the bar door swung open melodramatically and someone entered. All versification came to an abrupt halt as they made their way to the bar.

'That's...'

'Shush. Just watch.'

The bartender tugged their forelock.[20]

'High Poet, we're honoured.'

'Keep your voice down,' hissed the High Poet.

The bartender nodded but it was clear he was waiting for something more.

The High Poet sighed and threw out the second half of the expected couplet.

'Don't cast my name about the town.'

The bartender clapped.

'Wonderful. Just wonderful.'

The High Poet gave a half-hearted bow then got down to business.

'My guests. Have they arrived?'

'They're waiting for you. In the usual room.'

A clutch of coins were scattered onto the bar.

'Then let your best ale fill thy cups. Each *silent* soul will this night sup.'

The crowd, though still awed by the great man's appearance, quickly got the message and began to form an orderly queue at the bar.

'That one was quite good,' the High Poet observed, 'I must be feeling inspired.'

Then he walked briskly across the room, opened a small door and disappeared into the deeper recesses of the building.

'What was all that about?' asked Ella. 'Who is he meeting?'

'I think we both know.'

---

20. A small hat, made from a velvet-like fabric and worn by Othrysian barkeeps as a mark of respect. History does not record what for.

Ella took this in, then raised and drained her glass. It was one thing to talk about all-powerful entities, quite another to be sat next door to them.

'Should we stop him?'

'We will. But not here. And not now. I just wanted you to understand that the Gods are not the only obstacles in our way. They never are.'

Chapter Six

That night, no one slept well. Several of them sang nervous, verging on histrionic, ballads. Even after Bellboy and Gren returned from the Arena to say that the psychic stimulation field had been successfully smuggled into place.

But now, in the light of day, there was a genuine sense that the troops had been rallied and the fight was anyone's for the taking. If everyone could manage to get through the next hour or so without passing out, vomiting or fleeing from the building, things might just work out.

It was a story that had been played out in a million wings of a million stages.

Backstage at the Great Arena, the Songs of the Unsung prepared for their debut.

*

'You lot had better be good,' Gregoria cautioned the group. 'I've had a look at the crowd and they seem... judgemental.'

'We entrust our fates to the Muses,' said Bellboy.

They had all donned Othrysian poet robes, in the hopes that it might endear them to the audience or, failing that, confuse them long enough for the field to do its work. They looked like the members of a religious order whose recruitment standards had dropped.

'Just be prepared to duck There's a food stall out front doing deals on your heavier fruits and vegetables.'

This thought appeared to please her enormously, and Gregoria exited, grinning.

Ella felt a small bubble of panic forming in her gut.

'You know I've never sung in front of people before.'

'We have heard your voice,' The Band reminded her. 'It is adequate.'

'Thanks a lot. Also, pretty sure that was the stimulation field.'

'And it will be again,' Bellboy assured her. 'You'll be wonderful.'

'Or, at very least, adequate.'

The High Poet swept in on a wave of excited backstage chatter.

'Hallo, hallo. Just wanted to say I am very much looking forward to your performance. I wish you whatever your personal belief systems demand. Good fortune, fractured limbs...'

He cast an eye over the assembled Unsung.

'Where is young master Delios?'

'He is unwell,' snapped Ella, to a cautionary glance from Bellboy.

The High Poet was perturbed, thought Ella. Possibly even a little afraid. But you didn't get to be High Poet of Othrys without a knack for dissemblance.

'That is a shame. He was once such a promising talent, you know. But the pressure got to him. Poetry can be a cruel mistress.'

'We all have our weaknesses,' said Bellboy.

'That we do. Mine has always been fame. It's difficult to admit – and I'll prevail upon you never to repeat it – but the words never mattered as much to me as the applause. The acclaim. I suppose that's why I'm the High Poet and Delios is...'

'An artist,' said The Band.

The High Poet shuddered.

'I hope you don't wish such ill on all of your friends. Still, I had hoped he'd found a new outlet. After his free verse group so sadly fell apart. Ah, well. I suppose we shall have to pray for a miracle.'

'I suppose we will,' agreed Bellboy.

'But to which God? That is the question.'

*

Delios sat at his desk, in his cabin, scratching words onto paper with an unusual level of ferocity.

Even in his altered state, he felt frustrated at being left out of his own salvation. Somewhere on the ship, he was half-aware, lay the unconscious form of the man he once was. And on the planet outside, his friends were working to make them one.

In brief flashes of lucidity, he cursed the fact he was of no use to them in that endeavour. Rather, he would be a distraction, a deterrent even.

87

It was a terrible time to start hearing voices.

'Delios, my child. Sitting in your cabin, so lonely. Scratching out poems like a rat scratches the bars of its cage.'

It was a deep, dark, sepulchral voice that came from everywhere and nowhere. It also, Delios decided, clearly imaginary and therefore could be ignored.

A second voice attempted to change his mind.

'Don't ignore us, Delios. You must heed us. Your friends need you.'

He barely paused in his writing, though his hand began to shake.

'A voice within, not without,' he whispered, 'Madness weeping for itself.'

A third voice now, gnawing at him.

'They are in great danger. You must go to them.'

'No. No. Must block them out. Must let my words build up to a shout.'

He leant into the page in front of him, writing faster and faster, until the pen snapped in his grip.

Then the three voices spoke in chorus.

'YOU WILL GO.'

*

The show had been, by any objective measure, a success. Artistically, it was a triumph. The songs were accessible, memorable and loaded with meaning. The performances were electric, eclectic and humane. The between song banter was genuinely witty but didn't wear out its welcome.

The applause was like gunfire. And from an audience made up largely of poets who, historically, hate anything that isn't their own work and aren't too fond of most of that.

Ella, The Band and Bellboy exited the stage feeling loved, appreciated and desperate to do it all over again.

'That was... I mean... I never...'

'It felt good to sing again.'

'If the Gods didn't hear that, they are no Gods at all.'

Ella took a deep breath and felt the field's effect begin to dissipate.

'Did it work though?'

'Let's back to the ship and find out,' said Bellboy.

The clapping and whooping that had carried them from the stage had died down on their exit, but now it began anew.

'Sorry, what's happening now?'

'An encore, apparently. Just not by us.'

*

The High Poet rode the wave of applause that had greeted his arrival with mock humility.

'The chorus have their place, I say! But verse alone will have its day.'

The assembled poets, who had only just recently been in total thrall to the Songs of the Unsung, cheered as if they had been released from captivity.

'And so, to soothe the beast in us. Our very own son, Delios!'

*

Backstage, Bellboy's face crashed.

'Oh no.'

Ella was struggling to hear over the noise of the crowd.

'What? What's happening?'

'Delios is here,' said The Band.

Bellboy growled with frustration.

'Somehow, they found him. They found him and brought him here.'

'Our Delios?' asked Ella. 'Or Past Delios?'

'I think we're about to find out.'

'But,' said The Band, 'if he fails here, as he did before...'

'Then everything we've done will be for nothing.'

*

Onstage, Delios stepped gingerly to the edge of the stage and looked out over an audience of his peers. The very same people who had cast him out, who had made him feel worthless, who had broken him, transformed him into prey for the Circus.

And through the haze of his fractured mind, he felt an overwhelming sense of love for them all. The poor, deluded fools. They didn't understand. How could they understand? Whatever they had done to him, they'd done from fear. Fear of their own failure.

As if sensing his thoughts, and undoubtedly responding to the fact that he had been staring at them in silence for at least a minute, the audience began to grow restless.

*

The boos and catcalls were even more intense than the applause had been.

'That is a shame,' said the High Poet smugly, walking off-stage from his fateful introduction.

'What have you done?' demanded Bellboy.

'The only thing I could.'

'Destroy a man?'

'Save a world.'

*

The crowd were now baying for blood.

Delios watched them going through the motions of outrage and was tempted to laugh. They really couldn't see it, couldn't even begin to comprehend the truth.

He had been designated a sacrifice. But he had survived. He – and at this point he became aware that he was thinking far more clearly than he had in a very long time – had friends, he had a purpose, he had hope for the future.

Not alone were those things to be cherished, he realised, but they were *everything.*

And man who has earned everything must be doing something right.

He opened his mouth and began to sing.

*

'The field's still active!' shouted Ella.

'Oh, please,' said Bellboy, calling on any non-malevolent deities that might be passing. 'Let him have this.'

Delios' confidence grew with every note. He had never felt so sure of anything. He was singing directly to every single member of the audience, crawling inside their hearts and embedding the message he so desperately needed them to hear:

'We can be better than this.'

And they responded in kind. Looking out, he saw hardened prose workers with tears in their eyes. Felt acrostics being concocted in his honour. The tingle of internal rhymes nuzzling at each other for comfort.

No God could compete with this.

He took all the words that had been crammed into his mind in that moment of theocratic cruelty and compressed them into music, the only container that could hold them.

And he set them free.

The hysterical cries of 'Delios!' that followed him from the stage would echo through the history of Othrys. He would be remembered as the poet who changed it all, who finally broke down the walls between poetry and song.[21]

But first, he had a score to settle.

'High Poet!'

The Delios that arrived backstage, lit from within by righteous fury, was not the man who had taken the stage minutes earlier. Nor was he the man currently being tended to aboard the Vanguard.

This was someone new.

Someone altogether more powerful.

---

21. And, in turn, created a lucrative new busking industry.

The High Poet turn a panicked step backwards, only to find Bellboy blocking his exit.

'How marvellous to see you again, my child,' he vamped as Delios grew closer. 'You did terribly well. *Terribly* well.'

'I don't think your friends will agree.'

The High Poet attempted flippancy.

'Friends? A poet has no friends, Delios. You should know that.'

Delios looked around the room. At Ella. At The Band.

'Then I am no poet.'

'We are always our own harshest critics.'

'Shall we test that hypothesis?'

'What do you want from me?'

Delios grabbed the High Poet by the scruff of his robe. They were face-to-face now.

'You were going to sacrifice one of your own. To them. For what?'

The older man seemed to crumple in his grasp.

'Them?' he said wearily. 'We're talking about Gods here. Not the damned Taxation Guild.'

'And that makes it better?'

'I had no choice. The Circus is coming! If I hadn't given them something, someone, they would have destroyed us. Our whole way of life.'

'Yes,' agreed Delios, releasing him in disgust. 'they would have. Utterly and completely. Thanks to my friends, perhaps they won't. But what I want to know is what did they offer you? What was worth the sanity of a poet and the freedom of a world?'

The High Poet had the decency to appear ashamed.

'They promised not to take what I already have. They wouldn't remove me from office when they were done with us. With you.'

'Then I'll offer you the same conditions. Turn the Circus away. Cancel their booking.'

'But they've already paid a deposit!'

'Turn the Circus away and you can remain a terrible poet in a thankless job for the rest of your days.'

The High Poet dug down deep and found a final scrap of resistance.

'Or?'

Delios' eyes glittered. But not with madness this time. With sanity.

'Or you will discover that my words are far from the only cutting thing in my arsenal.'

'I'm not usually a fan of wordplay, but I'll give you that one.'

'Have we an agreement?'

The greater the authority, the greater the defeat.

This was a rout.

'You have my word. And, just for good measure, another that very nearly rhymes with it.'

'You couldn't manage a good measure with a metronome,' spat Delios.

'New Delios is savage,' whispered Ella to The Band.

'We may need to give him an up-tempo number,' they agreed.

'Let him go.'

'Are you sure?' asked Bellboy.

'He's getting what he deserves. Self-knowledge. Just hope, for Othrys' sake, he doesn't decide to write a poem about it.'

'I wouldn't know where to start,' the High Poet admitted.

'Good.'

The head of Othrys society looked very small as he crept past Ella and The Band towards the exit.[22]

The Songs of the Unsung broke into collective applause.

'Delios,' said Ella. 'That was brilliant.'

The poet shrugged.

'The show went on, as it must.'

Bellboy grabbed him by the shoulders and pulled him into a tight embrace.

'My friend. It is so good to see you back to your old self.'

Delios pulled free.

'Yes, my mind is finally clear.'

'I told you. I promised you it would be.'

'My mind is clear and I have a question.'

'What is it, my friend? Ask me anything.'

The poet took a protective step towards his friends before challenging Bellboy directly.

When he did, his voice was ice.

'Who are you and what you do want with us?'

---

22. Something he would later nominate as a turning point in his massively successful memoir in verse, *From On High*. Justice is a mixed bag, at best.

Interlude

Gods do not make plans in the way that other beings do. And it's not simply because they move in mysterious ways their wonders to perform. After all, one person's mysterious is another's downright odd. Nor is it because their version of taking minutes tends, inevitably, to lead to bloodshed.

No, the big difference lies in the level of arrogance involved. Gods plan only for success. They don't waste any of their infinite existences on considering what might go wrong or how it might be avoided. They assume their plan will work and therefore do precisely what they want to do when they want to do it. Which really makes it less of a plan and more of a tantrum.

Trouble is, in an expanding multiverse with an ever increasing number of deities, all of whom have different value systems, inclinations and demands, it's impossible for grandiose schemes to be enacted with impunity.

Add time travel into the equation and chaos begins to look downright desirable.

None of this is entirely their fault.[23] Omnipotence is an unnatural state; it's bound to have side effects.

On the other hand, greater knowledge is meant to lend greater perspective, so you might imagine that complete, overarching knowledge would have a similar, relative effect. Whereas, in practice, the opposite would appear to be true.

The Gods of Ragnarok are a perfect example.

As far as they were concerned, taking over a circus run by a ragtag group of hippies, weirdos and vagabonds was an absolutely foolproof way of gorging themselves on psychic energy and prolonging their dominance in an ever more fragmented corner of reality.

It simply never occurred to them, as it would have done to anyone operating below the level of godhood, that this was a very stupid idea and could *only* go wrong.

It would eventually take the intervention of someone whose own race occasionally behaved like Gods to bring the point home to them.

Or, at least, it should have done.

The short version of this is that Gods are not particularly bright.

Bless them.

---

23. Nor is it entirely *not* their fault.

Chapter Seven

Bellboy dreamt of Flowerchild.

They were running across the dusty surface of Segonax, towards the first glimmer of hope either had experienced in some time.

Exhaustion was beginning to set in.

'It must be around here somewhere,' gasped Bellboy, as they stumbled to a halt.

'We're going in the wrong direction, Bellboy,' replied Flowerchild. 'They'll find us.'

'I'm telling you. That was a ship crashing.'

'I believe you. But do you think they won't have heard it too? That the kites won't find it before we do?'

'It's a ship. Transport. You said it yourself. We're the only ones left to fight. We get off-world, we find help.'

Flowerchild looked at him. Into him. And he felt the same combination of emotions she had always engendered. Love, yes. But also fear. Fear that he had led this extraordinary woman to her doom.

'How far are we going to get in a crashed ship?' she was asking him now.

'I'll fix it.'

She brushed his cheek with one of her soft and gentle hands.

'You can't fix everything.'

'I can try.'

Bellboy looked up. The kites were circling again and there was a distant, incongruous sound of a motor and wheels grinding the earth.

He was seized by a momentary panic. This couldn't be all there was. This was not how their story was meant to end.

Flowerchild took his hand, squeezed it.

'I'll keep them occupied. You find that ship and I'll find you.' There was not a trace of doubt on her face, Bellboy noted. She chose and acted. That was who she was. The strongest of the two of them. By some distance.

He knew he couldn't change her mind, so he chose to make her proud instead.

'No silly risks?' he said, forcing a smile.

'No silly risks,' she echoed. 'Now, go!'

*

A burst of electronic noise dragged him back into the present.[24]

'Flowerchild!' he cried out.

But it was AJ's voice, over the intercom, that replied.

---

24. Depending on your perspective, of course.

'I'm sorry, Bellboy. It's only me.'

'Good morning, AJ.'

'Did you sleep?'

'Do I ever?'

'No, but I'll keep asking.'

Bellboy sat up and reached for the shirt flung over the chair at the foot of the bed.

'And I appreciate it. Have we reached orbit yet?'

'The short answer to that would be no.'

'And the long answer?'

'Would be that you should probably get up here.'

The sound of something heavy hitting something metal blasted through the intercom.

'Now-ish would be good.'

*

Six months had passed since the show on Othrys, though any lingering sense of celebration had long since faded.

Delios' accusations had rattled the entire crew and though they'd briefly tried to soldier on, nothing Bellboy had been able to offer in his defence had felt sufficient. It wasn't so much that they didn't trust him as that they knew they shouldn't. They were up against Gods. It was safer not to take things on faith.

As a gesture of goodwill, however, Bellboy had ceded authority of the mission to the poet, his previous self now returned to, they hoped, a Circus-free life. He still wasn't sure Delios had fully recovered but trusted that with Gren still in command of the Vanguard, there would always be somebody around with everyone's best interests at heart.

Morale had, nonetheless, taken a hit.

'And I think they've made it perfectly clear how they feel about it!' Gren shouted, stomping across the bridge towards the console.

'I have taken that into consideration.'

'And ignored it completely, Delios!'

'It's the only way.' Delios was sitting in the usually empty pilot's chair next to AJ's station, wearing an unflappable expression that was begging to be surgically removed.

'It is not the only way. It's *your* way. And that's the point. You get a bee in that until-recently-scrambled bonnet of yours, and it doesn't matter what anyone else says...'

'That is an unfair accusation. I am doing my utmost to...'

'Stop it! Both of you!' yelled Ella. She was leaning wearily against the arm of Gren's command chair, as she had been for the twenty or so minutes this argument had been raging.

'Delios,' she said, 'no one is saying that you haven't done a fantastic job.'

'I am,' insisted Gren.

'No, you're not. I mean, look what we've accomplished in the last six months. The writer's strike on Blini-Gaar. The chorister uprising on Marpesia. Not to mention the charity drive to re-terraform the Boriatic Wastes. Eight billion people saw that show!'

'Thank you, Ella' said the poet, resisting the urge to stick his tongue out at the Captain.

'We're succeeding. Changing the timeline. Keeping the Circus away from those worlds.'

'Precisely. Whis is why...'

'We should carry on exactly as we have been!' exploded Gren. 'If the Band aren't ready to go home, then there are plenty of other worlds to save.'

Delios shook his head. How could he make them see?

'AJ?'

'Yes, Delios?'

'Could you please call up the most recent temporal tracking report?'

'Of course.'

The soft hum of reports being processed emanated from the navigation station.

'There's no point asking her!'

'And why is that, Captain?' asked Delios.

'She'll say whatever you want her to say. She has a crush on you.'

'I beg your pardon?'

'Call yourself a bloody poet and you can't even tell when a sentient patch of rust is pining away for you.'

AJ was incensed.

'I am not pining.'

'If you were pining any harder, you'd be a forest.'

If the Captain had hoped to flummox Delios, they'd succeeded admirably.

'Look, I was never really that kind of poet. I did the intricacies of leaves, that sort of thing.'

'I simply think,' said AJ, 'that Delios has demonstrated a real gift for leadership since Bellboy stepped down and that we should encourage him wherever possible.'

'Thank you, AJ. I appreciate your support.'

'Also, he has beautiful eyes.'

'Okay, let's not get sidetracked.'

'What colour would you call that, Delios? I want to say azure...'

'Besides,' added Ella, desperate to change the subject, 'Bellboy didn't step down. He was...'

A familiar hydraulic whoosh interrupted her.

'Deposed,' said Bellboy, stepping onto the bridge. 'Yes, I think we all remember that.'

Gren growled.

'What are you doing up here?'

'AJ invited me.'

'What colour are *your* eyes?'

'Why?'

'I think she may have a type.'

Flowerchild's face floated back into his mind.

'You can't fix everything,' she had said.

And what had he replied?

He could try.

'Out of curiosity, what *does* the most recent temporal tracking report say?'

'The Circus is still on a course to reach its final destination of Segonax,' said AJ sadly.

It wasn't the news anybody wanted to hear.

'How is that even possible?'

'Every time we change the timeline, they nip into the nearest system, find another inhabited planet, and set up shop there.'

'So,' said Gren, 'we're not accomplishing anything.'

'We're saving people,' Ella reminded them.

'And dooming others.'

'Yes, Bellboy,' said Delios darkly, 'Strange, isn't it? How your plan appears to have strengthened the Circus rather than weakening it...'

'Do we have to do this again?'

'You still haven't explained yourself.'

'I don't have an explanation.'

Delios was standing now, shaking with fury.

'I remembered you. I remembered all that time together in the Circus, side by side. Until my mind was freed.'

'You're welcome, by the way.'

'Still, I was willing to put it aside. Chalk it up to a side effect.'

'And then we misjudged our arrival on Boromeo,' chipped in AJ.

'Stop helping!' ordered Gren.

'The Circus,' said Delios, 'was already there. But you weren't.'

'I don't understand why we're still arguing about this. We're doing surgery on time with what amounts to a claw hammer. There are bound to be aberrations.'

'I acknowledge that. But *if* you are who you say you are, you'll accept that we need to be careful. The Old Gods are not an adversary we can afford to underestimate.'

'You got what you wanted, Delios. You're in charge. What more can I do?'

'You agreed you'd keep to your cabin.'

'I have! But, AJ...'

Gren couldn't resist.

'...missed you too damned much.'

The navigator gave a squeak of protest.

'We were at an impasse, Captain.'

'And it appears you still are,' said Bellboy. 'And whatever you think of me, I still want to help. So what's the problem?'

Delios shut his eyes. He was rapidly approaching his wit's end and having seen what lay beyond that was in no hurry to travel any further

'We need to go to Cinethon.'

'Then let's go to Cinethon.'

'The Band have refused.'

'What? Why?'

'They're afraid,' said Ella.

'Understandable.'

'Is it?' queried Gren. 'They've shared their whole existence since the Circus did... that to them. Do any of us really understand what it would be like to lose that connection?'

'I don't think it's just that,' said Ella. 'If we go to Cinethon...'

AJ completed her thought.

'...we must go when the Circus is already in residence, just before the members of the Band auditioned.'

'Why?' asked Bellboy.

'We must deal with all four of them at once – in a single moment or we risk the timelines branching beyond our control.'

'Therefore,' said the Captain, 'this is the last stand before Segonax. The Band's feelings aside, I'm not convinced we're ready either.'

Bellboy stroked his chin.

'We may have to be. Do you want me to talk to them?'

'Honestly,' said Ella, 'it might help.'

Delios exploded with frustration.

'Is *no one* listening to me? We don't know if we can trust him. He could be working for them.'

'We're talking about Gods,' barked Gren. 'Any of us could be working for them.'

'Is that intended to make me feel better?'

'Delios,' said Ella, 'we either leave them to it, and run the risk of the Circus getting to Segonax unscathed, or we let Bellboy try to convince them.'

'To be or not to be. That is the question. Whether 'tis nobler in the mind to suffer the slings and arrows of outrageous fortune, or to take arms against a sea of troubles and by opposing end them.'

An awkward silence settled over the bridge. Regardless of one's planet of origin, random bursts of Shakespeare[25] were never a good sign.

'Delios,' asked AJ gently, 'are you feeling all right?'

'I am quite well, thank you.' He looked at each of the disbelieving faces in turn. 'What? I'm still a poet.' He sighed and turned to Bellboy. 'Fine. Try to make them understand.'

'I'll do my best.'

'This doesn't mean you're back in charge.'

'I never assumed it did.'

'Very well.'

---

25. The power of parallel evolution had ensured that variations on William Shakespeare and his works had cropped up on thousands of worlds. Except for the few that had a Christopher Marlowe.

Bellboy nodded and headed for the exit, exchanging only the slightest glance of concern with Gren as he went.

Delios watched him go.

'To die,' he whispered, 'to sleep.'

Chapter Eight

As Bellboy made his way towards The Band's cabin, he swore he could hear music. Not the field-generated, fully arranged variety to which he had become accustomed, but a faint humming, a short series of notes repeated on a loop.

It grew louder as he approached the cabin door, obviously emanating from within. There was something unsettling about it, as though he were hearing the soundtrack to somebody's soul. Not the secrets that tumbled out when their inhibitions were lowered, but the secrets that even they didn't know they kept.

He reached out to press the buzzer next to the door and the sound stopped abruptly. As if his presence had been sensed.

The door slid open, revealing The Band sitting upright on their bunk.

'Bellboy. Welcome to our cabin, as ever. Have you been liberated?'

He stepped into the room cautiously.

'After a fashion.'

'This is good.'

'Is it?'

The Band hesitated before continuing.

'I do not think that Delios is handling command as well as everyone pretends.'

'I'm sure he's doing his best.'

'Of this we have no doubt.'

'What about you? How are you handling things?'

It had always been difficult to read The Band's facial expressions. They never settled for long enough. But it seemed to Bellboy that they were currently even more enigmatic than usual.

'We are... anxious.'

'Can I help?'

Each of the four voices cracked in a slightly different place. Bellboy felt his own heart lurch.

'They wish us to go to Cinethon.'

He sat next to them on the bunk and took their hand.

'That was always the plan,' he said softly.

'Yes. But it is possible we did not fully consider the ramifications.'

'You're worried about being separated?'

'Perhaps.'

'I'm sorry. I wish I could say I know what you're going through, but I don't.'

The Band stood and tried to pace. The room, however, was far too small and they ended up walking in a series of upsettingly tight concentric circles. Bellboy had never seen them this agitated. Or, really, agitated at all.

'We don't even know our names,' they said piteously.

'Sorry?'

'We know we were four, but we have no true memory of who we – they – were. Our names. Our families. Our lives. All gone. What does the universe hold for four people without a past? Without identity?'

Bellboy patted the bunk, inviting them to sit again. They declined.

'It might all come back.'

'Delios forgot much when he was healed.'

'He forgot *me*,' said Bellboy remorsefully.

'We do not wish to forget you. When we joined the circus, we were alone. You and Flowerchild did not treat us as the others did, as something to be avoided, to be feared.'

Bellboy kept his voice even, determined not to make this about himself. But he knew he was holding back tears for which he would soon have to make time.

'That was Flowerchild, far more than me. She never had to try to be kind. She just was. It was in her bones.'

He became very aware of The Band watching him.

'Do you think you will find her if we get to Segonax?' they asked finally.

Bellboy interrogated himself. Did he think that? Or was that something he would say to convince The Band to go along with his plan? Was that who he had become?

Was it justice he sought or vengeance?

110

'It's the only place left I can think to look,' he said, certain this was the truth. 'She seems to have vanished from the rest of the timeline.'

'And we must go to Cinethon before we go to Segonax?'

'Yes.'

The Band sat. Folded their hands in their lap.

'Then we will go to Cinethon.'

'Are you sure?'

The Band tried to smile. They didn't quite manage it, not on all four faces, but the effort was appreciated.

'We would like to feel we too had kindness in our bones.'

Bellboy found himself moved beyond what he had anticipated.

'Thank you.'

'You will tell Delios?'

'Of course. If you want me to.'

'We would do so ourselves but we have developed the urge to strike him of late.'

The laughter was kindly intended but Bellboy tried to stem it all the same. He failed.

'Quite firmly would be our preference. We are sure it will pass but we would like to avoid that eventuality.'

'Of course,' managed Bellboy, having finally caught his breath.

'For the sake of kindness.'

'For the sake of kindness,' he agreed.

*

Delios stumbled into his cabin, his heart racing and his mouth dry. The door slid shut behind him with its usual gentility but, nonetheless, he jumped, banging his shoulder painfully against the wall of the confined space.

It was all coming apart. The mind he had fought so hard to reclaim was splintering.

'Blind,' he mumbled frantically 'All blind. The path hard to find. The ties that must bind. The clock that unwinds.' The words were tumbling out of him, each quicker than the last, as though some unseen force was flinging them from his mouth with all their strength.

'No,' he said firmly, gripping the back of the nearby chair and squeezing it until his knuckles turned white. 'I will not be lost again. I am found. I am *found*.'

He was already singing before he heard the music.

The song that fell from Delios' heart was a confused patchwork of images in a minor key. There was none of the catharsis of his performance on Othrys, though it came from a deeper well. Beauty and repugnance in unison. Terror and resignation. Melody tied around the handle of an atonal knife.

He screamed out the final notes just as the buzzer sounded at his door. Fell back against the door controls. And collapsed as Bellboy stepped into the room.

'Delios, I just wanted to...'

Bellboy rushed to his friend, now writhing and weeping on the deck, lodged between the wall and the unforgiving bunk. He grabbed him and pulled him up into a sitting position.

'What is it? What's wrong?'

The poet whimpered in his arms.

'It's going wrong, Bellboy. The wrong song. Sung by those who don't belong. I don't belong. Why don't I belong?'

'It's all right,' his friend told him, hoping it was true. He rocked him gently, like an anguished child. 'We're going to Cinethon. And we're going to finish this.'

*

The Garden City of Cinethon *does* appear on a number of lists. Usually found in the sort of magazines you find on short hop planetary journeys, offering suggestions for where the overwrought middle class business executive might find a little peace and quiet at an attractive price.[26]

And it's not a bad suggestion, although most business executives tended to go a bit stir crazy after forty-eight hours of the kind of peace and quiet to be found there.

In truth, it qualified for that old horror staple of 'quiet, too quiet'. There was no industrial noise or bustling crowds or barking entrepreneurs. But there was also no bird song, no trees rustling gently in the wind, no crickets chirping romantically in the glow of an improbable sunset.

It was beautiful. It was pristine. And it was silent.

The heavy clunk of the Vanguard's hatch felt like an explosion. The clank of footsteps as Ella, The Band, Bellboy and Delios descended the ramp were gunshots in a nursery.

---

26. *Modern Being's* 'Ten Destinations to Prevent An International Incident' being one example.

'Oh my,' said Ella, 'it's gorgeous.'

She was right. Bare rolling hills of a deep rust red rose and fell in every direction, the sky above them a pale, crystal blue. Two suns, one slightly higher than other, cast layered rays that felt like an exhibition laid on for tourists.

'Cinethon is known for its beauty,' said The Band. Their voices remained impassive, but it was obvious that being home was the subject of mixed emotions. More mixed than even a four-person gestalt entity ordinarily experienced. 'And its tranquillity,' they added.

'Like the Eye of Orion?'

A little hometown pride seemed to creep into The Band's dismissal of this comparison.

'The Eye of Orion is largely uninhabited. Its tranquillity is no achievement. On Cinethon, the people are peaceful, and the world follows suit.'

'All the more reason,' stressed Bellboy, 'to prevent the Circus from getting its tent pegs into them.'

Delios had rallied since his recent episode, but he still sounded subdued.

'I don't remember it being so quiet.'

'You were here, with the Circus?' asked Ella. 'First go round, I mean?'

'I think so.'

'It's getting harder to tell, isn't it?' suggested Bellboy.

Delios appeared to take this as a rebuke. 'I remember the day the Band joined us,' he snapped, 'it's just... a little out-of-focus.'

'That bit is terribly clear for me.'

'It sounds ridiculous when I say it out loud, but I thought it would be a planet of singers or something... Like Othrys and the poets.'

The Band looked suddenly stricken.

'We are afraid there is no music on Cinethon.'

'*No* music?'

'We have no native capacity for it.'

'But you?'

'I believe that we – those we once were – were exceptions to the rule. That each of us discovered music in our own way. Travellers in the spaceports. Off-world visitors, in the streets, whistling to pass the time. History books that spoke of the battle hymns of our ancient enemies, before the Great Calm. Fragments, but intoxicating. But there was nowhere for us to take our passions. No one who cared to listen.'

'Nowhere but the Circus.'

'And each other. First, each other.'

'I thought,' said Bellboy, 'that you didn't remember your past selves.'

'We did not. But now we are here. Now we are home...'

'The melody returns, resolves.'

Bellboy touched Delios' arm.

'Are you sure you're up to this?'

The poet inclined his head.

'I wish to see it through.'

'Then,' said The Band, 'we must find the Circus.'

*

The Psychic Circus had been designed to be not only a circus in its own right, but the memory of all of the circuses that had preceded it. Wherever possible, it aimed to be defiantly lo-fi. Sure, there was the occasional robot pressed into the service, but it was all housed in traditional, multi-coloured tents, leading to an equally old school Big Top, containing a large, sawdust-covered ring, around which the local audience would gather to watch the astounding acts on offer.

In the smaller tent at its entrance, a meeting was taking place between its current proprietor and two of her staff.

One was a young poet by the name Delios, already having suffered the tender mercies of the Gods. Another was an extremely thin, preposterously tall creature in a battered top hat. The rest of his clothes, the battered long coat, the baggy trousers tied at the waist with string, had apparently been designed for several creatures of different sizes, none of whom were him.

His name was The Tooth. A fact most assumed was in sarcastic reference to the state of his dentistry before discovering, upon further investigation, that it appeared on his birth certificate.

The Tooth was not in a good mood. The Tooth was never in a good mood. Something, perversely, that brought him great joy.

'Ticket sales are down again, my lady,' he wheezed.

'All is quiet. Deathly quiet,' confirmed Delios, 'Not a mote of dust stirs or is stirred.'

The Tooth removed his hat, revealed a pate swarming with greasy black hair.

'To translate for my loquacious friend, the good people of Cinethon aren't biting. The whispering dullards aren't doing much of anything. It'd be easier to drum up excitement on a crypt ship.'

The woman to whom both addressed their remarks listened with patience, even kindness. Her long, curly blonde hair was piled into a convenient bun atop her head and she wore what had once been a cheerful, floral dress but was now streaked with grime and disappointment.

She was also visibly pregnant.

'When I took you on, Tooth,' said Flowerchild, 'you assured me you could sell fire to an Ice Warrior.'

The Tooth acknowledged this but offered what he thought an important qualification.

'Not a dead one, my lady. And that's pretty much what we're dealing with here. They're just all so damned placid. It's like the concept of entertainment is beyond them.'

Flowerchild rubbed her eyes. She was so tired these days. Something, she had no doubt, to do with the utter lack of sleep. Such a shame. She used to love sleep but it seemed to be beyond her now. The responsibilities of her role weighed on her, not to mention the fatigue inherent in where she found herself. And surpassing all that, her unborn child was growing increasingly restless. She didn't blame them, but it wasn't helping.

'We have... stockholders to whom we must account. And they are not fond of excuses.'

'The divine must be fortified. Glorified. Sanctified.'

'And so say all of us,' replied The Tooth. 'But unless we get some new acts in, some fresh blood, they're going begging. Which, as you say, doesn't do any of us any good.'

'And where are we going to get new acts? You've just finished telling me the populace are as wet as a Saturnyne weekend.'

The tent flap behind them rustled. The Tooth drew a small rusty blade from his belt.

'Maybe we can help with that,' said Ella, hoping that it had come off as slick and cool as she'd intended. 'We are the Songs of the Un...'

'Flowerchild!'

Bellboy shoved past her, completely oblivious to the unconscionable way in which he'd stepped on her lines.

Flowerchild too was overcome.

'Bellboy!'

They ran to each other and embraced. The commentary came thick and fast.

'What are you doing here?'

'I could ask you the same thing!'

'I've looked everywhere for you.'

'Might have been easier not to leave me in the first place.'

'That's hardly fair.'

'No, but I've been waiting to say it for a long time.'

Ella turned to the Band, resigned to her moment having been nicked.

'I take it that's Bellboy's lost love.'

'Yes,' said The Band, 'Although, she is larger than we remember.'

'Seriously?'

'We are quite serious. She certainly had significantly fewer bumps.'

Ella laughed.

'You'd think four minds would be sharper than one. She's clearly pregnant.'

Having taken a potshot at The Band's reasoning skills, she was deeply embarrassed at how long it took for the implications of that revelation to strike her.

'Oh,' she said.

Bellboy had done better than 'oh' but not by much. 'You're...'

'Yes,' said Flowerchild. 'And if you ask if it's yours, I will ask my associate here to hit you with something heavy. And sharp.'

The Tooth found himself wishing Bellboy to tempt fate.

'It would be my pleasure, my lady.'

'But where have you been,' Bellboy asked, 'I've been up and down the timeline searching for you since I left you on Segonax.'

'Segonax?' Flowerchild seemed genuinely confused.

The Tooth, a full service factotum, leaned in.

'Our next stop, my lady.'

'Of course.' Bellboy all but slapped his own forehead. 'You haven't been there yet. But that means...'

'I've been on my own for the last six months since you disappeared. On Othrys.'

'You weren't on Othrys.'

'If we weren't together on Othrys,' Flowerchild insisted, 'then this baby may have a future as a religious leader.'

'A blessed even, between the tents.'

'Careful Past Delios,' said Bellboy. 'I mean, Delios. Hello. Good to... see you again.'

This wasn't right, he thought. They had saved Delios, prevented him from meeting his fate. Why was he still with the Circus? And still damaged?

'Have you two met?'

'On... Othrys?' Time travel really was a bear when it came to making small talk.

Flowerchild moved away from Bellboy, suspicion etched on her beautiful face. He felt his heart break a little.

'Delios came to us after your disappearance. What is going on, Bellboy?'

Ella decided to mount a rescue.

'Sorry to interrupt, but I have a question.'

'And who's she?' asked Flowerchild. 'Traded in for a younger model, have you?'

Ella retched.

'Ewww. No.'

'There is a marked resemblance,' said The Tooth, eyeing Ella in a way that made her wish she had a brick.

'To whom?' asked Flowerchild.

'To you, my lady.'

'I don't see it,' said Ella and Flowerchild together.

It was Bellboy's turn to intervene.

'What was your question, Ella?'

'This is the Psychic Circus, yes?'

'Of course,' said Flowerchild.

'The Greatest Show in the Galaxy,' added The Tooth luridly. 'Not that you'd know it, from the box office.'

'And, you, Flowerchild, you're in charge of it?'

'That is a good question,' said The Band.

Everyone was now looking at everyone else with varying degrees of doubt. The Tooth's knife twitched in his grubby hand.

'And there's a good answer,' insisted Flowerchild. 'But we can't talk here.'

*

Delios, which is to say present day Delios, as opposed to the current Past Delios (who had now superseded the previous Past Delios as a way of confusing the whole Delios question) crept warily around the back of the circus tents.

He was carrying a large metallic container and had a communicator pinned to his chest, through which Gren was offering what they obviously assumed to be helpful interjections.

'How are we doing?'

The poet bristled.

'I am doing fine.'

'It wasn't an accusation.'

'No. Nothing ever is. And yet, you feel the need to keep electronic tabs on what is an insultingly simple assignment.'

'We're worried about you, you miserable...'

'Of course you are. Delios is weak. He's broken. He's a *poet* and, as such, can't possibly be expected to accomplish anything sensible or *help* in any way.'

As if to punctuate the thought, he set down the container, opened its lid and began to the remove the components stored within.

'No one has said anything of the sort. Although, to be fair, you *are* a poet.'

'And you write beautifully.'

'AJ! Don't get involved.'

'There's no cause to speak to her in that manner.'

'Thank you, Delios.'

'I can't win,' said Gren.

Delios was now fixing the long pointy bits of metal at his disposal to the larger, flatter bits of different metal.

'Now you understand my predicament,' he said.

'I take it you've found a suitably place to install the stimulation field.'

Delios looked at the service access point he had located, a short distance away from the main tents. It was covered in the same striped canvas and was essentially a wooden frame, built around and for the protection of the Circus' backup generator.

'Yes. And I'll have it installed momentarily if you'd let me get on with it.'

'That's fine then. Check in if you need anything. Gren out.' The signal cut out passive-aggressively, which was a trick that only the most experienced starship captains could pull off.

Delios finished assembling the stimulation field device, attached it to the generator via two short pieces

122

of wire and tucked it out of sight behind a canvas flap.

'Task, taken to,' he murmured. 'A mask unglued.'

He said something altogether less poetic a moment later, when Ella and The Band appeared unexpectedly from behind the tents. Primarily as he had immediately leapt to his feet and then fallen over his own container, landing in an undignified heap on the ground.

Strangely enough, it did not improve his mood.

'Are you almost finished?' Ella enquired, trying desperately not to smirk.

'Metre's measure,' he spat, struggling to his feet and ineffectually attempting to brush dirt from his robes. 'Are you all actively conspiring against me?'

'Not to the best of our knowledge,' said The Band.

'Then you have missed your calling. Now, where's Bellboy? The stimulation field is in place so I suggest we act as soon as is feasible.'

Ella grimaced.

'About that...'

'What is it now?'

'We ran into a... complication.'

*

Bellboy and Flowerchild walked through one of the countless elegant, tranquil and thoroughly interchangeable gardens of Cinethon. It felt bizarre, unreal, after so much wishing and searching, to be, once again, in each other's company. There was so much to talk about; both struggled to find the words.

It didn't help matters that The Tooth trailed in their wake, a few paces behind, like a distracted child or overprotective pet.

'I still can't quite believe it.' Bellboy knew he was stating the obvious but it was no less true for being trite.

'Nor can I.'

'I hadn't found the strength to admit it to myself but I think I had almost given up hope.'

'I really thought you'd run away.'

'I'm sorry.'

'No. I was happy for you. You'd made it out.' She patted her belly meaningfully. 'Of course, I didn't know about our newest collaboration then.'

As much as Bellboy had struggled to process Flowerchild's reappearance, it was nothing compared to the blown synapses elicited by the thought of their child.

'How long?' he asked.

'A month more. Maybe two.'

Bellboy lowered his voice, suddenly aware of The Tooth trying a little too hard to seem disinterested.

'I'll get you out of here.'

'It's not as simple as that.'

'My lady?' called The Tooth, as if reading their minds. Bellboy was struck by a sudden thought. This was the Psychic Circus after all. For all he knew, the horrid little man actually could read minds.

'Yes, Tooth?'

He broke into a small, stumbling run until he was level with them.

'Just a reminder that...'

'What is it?' asked Bellboy.

'We are never quite alone, sir.'

This time, Bellboy's whisper was for everyone's benefit.

'The Gods.'

'Yes,' said Flowerchild.

'I don't understand. What happened?'

The idea of Flowerchild working for the Gods of Ragnarok went so completely against his concept of her as to be unbelievable. But then he hadn't been a time travelling song and dance man when this had all started. People changed.

'A process of elimination.'

He looked deeply into her eyes, a place where he had only ever found comfort, and was rewarded with little but his own reflection.

'I'm sorry, I don't...'

Flowerchild began to walk faster, as though she might escape her own story. Bellboy matched her pace, while The Tooth returned to the rearguard.

'The Gods' influence over the Circus had been getting stronger,' she told him. 'We could all feel it. Every planet felt a step closer to their presence. But then things began to go wrong. We'd show up on worlds and discover we weren't expected. Or welcome.'

Bellboy felt strangely guilty.

'That may be partly our fault.'

'In any case, there was plenty of blame to go round. And, somehow, they always found a way to distribute it. Until, eventually, there were very few of us left.'

'I'm sorry. I truly am.'

As if answering his unspoken question, Flowerchild continued:

'I wanted to resist, but... the child. Our child. I couldn't risk it. And I suppose I hoped you would show up and save the day. If I just held my nerve.' She stopped and faced him. 'Tell me, my love. Have you shown up to save the day?'

'I'd rather we saved the day together.'

'I don't know if I can. The Gods want new acts.'

Bellboy frowned. Something new was bothering him.

'How do you know that? Do they speak to you?'

'In a way. Sometimes, I dream of them. Sometimes a thought just arrives in my head, and I know it's them. Their voices are louder now.'

Flowerchild adored Bellboy. Had done since the moment she had first laid eyes on him. But he was a man of habit and had seldom surprised her. He did so now.

'Well, then. In that case, I suppose we had best get them some new acts.'

'Really?'

'Do you trust me?'

'Implicitly.'

Bellboy laughed, loudly and from the gut, surprising Flowerchild for the second time.

'I remember you being smarter than that.'

'And I remember you being less...'

'Excitable?'

126

'That's one word for it.' She called out to her shadow with an authority in her voice that she had always possessed but rarely employed.

'Tooth!'

'Yes, my lady?'

'Put out the word. Auditions begin tomorrow.'

Once again, The Tooth lolloped up to them. He seemed doubtful.

'I'm not sure we'll get much response.'

'We'll get four,' Bellboy promised. 'That much I can guarantee.'

'You heard the man.'

'Yes, my lady.'

Flowerchild dismissed The Tooth with a flick of her head. He gave a stiffly mannered bow and slunk away.

Finally, they were alone.

'I should get back too,' she said.

'Of course.'

Flowerchild closed the gap between herself and the man she loved until they were almost touching, the way they used to, each an extension of the other.

'Tell me it will work. Whatever it is you're planning.'

'It will work.'

'I believe you.' She grinned and placed her hand on Bellboy's chest, over his rapidly beating heart. 'I guess you're right. I used to be smarter.'

*

'This is troubling news,' said Delios, deep in thought. Ella had explained everything they'd witnessed so far, including the presence of yet another broken version of the poet.

They had retreated to a safe distance from the Circus and now sat on the crest of a crimson hillock, overlooking the nearby gardens.

'Why? I mean, why is it more troubling than any of the other extremely troubling things that have happened today alone?'

'You say that I am here. My past self. With the Circus.'

'Yes.'

'What of it?' asked The Band.

'I shouldn't be. Not after our interference on Othrys. Also, I have no memory of Flowerchild. Or this Tooth creature. And when you joined us on the Vanguard, Band, you claimed never to have met me.'

'The timelines must be in flux.'

'That has become a convenient excuse.'

'Doesn't stop it being true,' Ella pointed out.

But Delios wasn't really listening anymore. He was putting together an enormous jigsaw puzzle in his head and he didn't need anyone claiming to have found another bit of sky.

'It doesn't matter. Don't you see? Nothing is happening as it did before. No one is where they were.'

'Which is what we wanted,' said The Band.

'But we've gone too far. Changed too much.'

Ella could feel her last vestige of comprehension begin to slip away.

'That's ridiculous,' she asserted. 'We haven't changed nearly enough.

'When you saved me on Othrys, we were changing an outcome we understood. The timeline was still largely unaltered. If this happened, then that would happen. But we have no compass now. No map against which to measure our interference.'

'I hate time travel.'

'On that we agree.'

'We see him,' said The Band, who had been keeping watch on the gardens below.

Sure enough, even at a distance, Bellboy's bright yellow jacket and purple pantaloons stood out like a rescue flare.

Ella jumped up and waved frantically.

'We have communicators,' The Band reminded her.

Bellboy spotted her and waved back.

'Sometimes,' she said, 'it pays to do things the old-fashioned way.

*

On the way back to the ship, Delios outlined his concerns once more, but Bellboy seemed unmoved.

'None of that matters.'

'But we're in the dark, Bellboy. Completely in the dark.'

'Then we move towards the light. We concentrate on what we do know. Our friend here is going to be hurt and we are going to stop it.'

'It will be soon,' said The Band with a shiver. The longer they were on Cinethon, the more anxious they became. The less *together* they became. Even their voices had begun to lose cohesion, their words no longer entirely in sync.

'You see? That's what we should be focused on.'

'You're talking about battles, Bellboy,' Delios argued. 'I'm talking about the war.'

'You're talking about fear, Delios. And I'm talking about destiny.'

Ella let out a grunt of annoyance.

'We can talk,' she said. 'Or we can do. I vote for do.'

'Ella's right,' said Bellboy. 'This is no time to argue amongst ourselves. We have an audition to prepare for.'

'That,' said Delios, 'and the potential destruction of all of space and time.'

'That too.'

*

'You were marvellous, my lady,' crowed The Tooth, dancing a small private jig around the tent.

'Please be quiet,' said Flowerchild. She chewed on her thumbnail as she paced. 'I'm trying to think.'

But her delighted drudge could not be silenced.

'It was the performance of a lifetime. He believed every word. The Gods will be pleased.'

Past Delios was sitting cross-legged in one corner, staring into the precise centre of the middle distance.

'Their joy drifts like smoke to an altar above. The sight and sense of all our love.'

The Tooth hooted.

'You see, my lady? Listen to our good friend Delios. You're an inspiration.'

Flowerchild wheeled to face him.

'I don't want to do this.'

All the pleasure drained from The Tooth's tone, leaving a nasty promise in its wake.

'But you have no choice. You made a promise in exchange for the safety of your child. Of his child. He'll understand. He'll love you for your sacrifice.'

'Haven't I sacrificed enough?'

The Tooth grinned horribly.

'Oh, but that's the beauty of sacrifice. It's the gift that keeps on giving.'

*

'I'm happy for you, you know.'

The lights in the Vanguard corridors had been dimmed to a soft glow in order to, according to Gren, approximate the local day/night cycle and to save power. AJ maintained it was purely because the Captain liked the effect.

'Thank you, Ella,' said Bellboy.

'No, I mean it. I know what it's like to dream of things being different. Of life being better. It's kind of breath-taking to see it actually happen for someone.'

Technically, they were both headed for their cabins and a good night's sleep, but they had been walking in circles for hours, killing what time they could before whatever tomorrow had in store for them.

'I'm sorry we can't change things for you. Your past, I mean.'

'But you have. Look, I still don't know why I'm here, why I got that invitation, or really – to be honest – why I accepted it. But I do know that before I joined this merry band of lunatics, I was just me. A part of nothing. That's not true anymore. Now, I...'

She drifted off.

'Are you okay?'

'Hmm? Oh, yes. Sorry. I thought I was going to burst into song for a moment there and I was conserving my voice.'

'Stimulation field's installed at the Circus now,' Bellboy reminded her.

'And yet...'

They both laughed. Bellboy felt a strange compulsion to wrap his arms around her and tell her everything was going to be all right.

He fought it.

'You should get back to your cabin,' he said. 'Get some sleep. Big day tomorrow. The command performance, I guess you could call it.'

'I will if you will.'

She really was like her, Bellboy thought. Stubborn and self-possessed. Endlessly curious and quite unstoppable.

'I suppose we could walk a little bit longer.'

*

The bridge of the Vanguard was as still as the nerve centre of a retrofitted time ship had any right to be. Lights flashed intermittently across panels, the only illumination in the faux night shadows. The occasional click or beep or whirr were the only sounds.

Gren's command chair sat empty. As did every other seat on offer. The ancient mariners of Earth might have called to mind tales of the *Mary Celeste*.[27] Which would have caused uproar amongst the even more ancient mariners of Elys VI, for whom the phrase *mary celeste* translated as a grave insult involving their mother's marital fidelity.

With its usual hiss and whoosh, the bridge door opened, admitting a set of footsteps and an almost inaudible hum.

'Hello?' said AJ groggily. Sentient patches of rust did not technically need sleep, but she'd heard such good things about it from the others that she'd given it a go. 'Hello? Is someone there?'

The humming grew louder and the footsteps nearer. It was still difficult to place the melody. It was a snatch of a tune, its first few notes, clipped and looped.

AJ switched on the overheard lights and breathed a sigh of relief.

'Oh,' she said, 'it's you. Can't sleep? I'm not surprised, considering...'

There was no reply but the humming took on a new edge, a vicious atonality eroding the repeated phrase.

On the navigator's chair lay a large metal spanner, an antiquated piece of equipment that Gren swore by and, often, at. Only hours ago, they had been attempting to repair a slight imbalance in the gyro control mechanism, which AJ knew was code for keeping themselves busy so as to avoid thinking.

A hand reached out and grasped the weighty tool. Raised it high.

---

27. Once, of course, they'd recovered from the nervous collapse caused by finding themselves in space.

'What are you doing?'

Hum. Hum. Hum.

'No, please. Stop.'

Hum. Hum. Hum. Hum. Hum.

'Please.'

The spanner crashed down on the console, sending a shower of sparks flying.

AJ screamed.

Chapter Nine

It was dawn on Cinethon and the Big Top of the Psychic Circus was already full to bursting. Regardless of The Tooth's misgivings, it seemed the planet's populace possessed some curiosity. He had, however, been proved right on one score. None of them showed any inclination to audition.

And it wasn't as if they were the most engaged crowd. Ordinarily, on audition days, the air sparked with excitement. Would someone's dreams come true? Or be crushed? Audiences differed on which they like more. The Tooth knew his preference, although job security demanded he keep that to himself.

This lot, however.

He twitched back the curtain that separated the entrance tent from the ring and watched them whisper blandly amongst themselves.

Some people just didn't know how to have fun.

Retreating to the box office, he found Flowerchild behind the ticket counter. She was pale and distracted. There remained a distinct lack of potential new recruits.

'What did I tell you? They're content to watch, but they're not looking to get involved.'

'Bellboy said...'

'Perhaps Bellboy lied to you. You did to him.'

'He wouldn't.'

The Tooth regarded her and felt, once again, mystified. She was so capable in so many was, but this sentimental streak was going to get her killed. Get them all killed.

'My lady. The list of things I once believed I would not do, has long been outstripped by the list of things I've done. That is the price of the Circus.'

'Just get on with it.'

'Get on with what? We haven't any volunteers.'

'They will come. Start the show.'

'As you wish, my lady.'

The Tooth straightened his top hat and tugged at his clothes. Neither action improved matters.

Then he strode into the ring.

*

Specks of scarlet dust floated eerily through the spotlight's beam. An emaciated young man, a snare drum hung around his neck on a narrow fabric strap, stepped forward and performed an introductory roll. He had been with the Circus for so long that neither he nor anyone else remembered his name.

The Tooth stepped into the light.

'Gentle people of Cinethon. Hear me now. This is a day amongst days.' He turned as he spoke, presenting his hundred watt smile to each segment of the audience in turn. 'One that will be marked, by the fortunate

136

amongst you, as the day when everything changed. The day when you joined the Psychic Circus.'

The denizens of Cinethon stared back at him. Applause wasn't really a feature of their lives. Too raucous by far.[28]

'Tough room,' he said, beneath his breath.

'Have you a light,' he continued, for the sake of professional pride, 'that you have hitherto hidden beneath the nearest bushel? A talent you have been too afraid to unveil? Do you have a turn? A trick? Something that makes you special?'

Again, silence. Just eyes locked on him, waiting for something to happen. The Tooth found himself double-checking that he was still clothed and that his mother was not lurking in the crowd, dressed as a fish.[29]

Then *she* appeared through the curtain, Flowerchild at her back. And the crowd, testing the limits of possibility, grew even more silent.

She was of average height and average build.[30] Her face was vaguely symmetrical and her hair had been styled to frame it in an adequate manner. Her dress had a length and a colour but neither really impressed themselves on the memory.

Encountered in the street, she would be passed by. Not because there was anything wrong with her but

---

28. Approval, on Cinethon, was generally displayed via a respectful silence. As were disapproval, ambivalence, elation and hunger.

29. Everyone's performance nightmares have their own twist.

30. For Cinethon, obviously. And it's still a purely statistical observation.

because there wasn't. Nothing about her, for better or worse, caught the eye.

So it was not her appearance that had stunned the crowd.

The young woman was humming. On a world without music that would have been startling enough. But it was the sheer quality of the sound that took the breath away. Even a Cinethon crowd, with so little frame of reference, knew they were experiencing something far beyond the ordinary.

Flowerchild shot the Tooth a look of vindication, which he accepted grudgingly.

The humming stopped as the woman reached The Tooth's side.

'Welcome, stranger,' he said. 'Welcome to the Psychic Circus. What is your name?'

'I am Mel'Dee of Cinethon. And I have come to sing for you.' Her speaking voice was somehow equally musical and she faced the crowd without fear. Challenging them.

A fresh round of whispers began and to The Tooth's surprise and satisfaction, it contained a ripple of genuine shock.

*

Gren walked onto the bridge, prepared to apologise. They had been unduly sharp with AJ the previous evening, although they still maintained they had been provoked. AJ was a fine navigator but Gren had been fixing gyro controls since they were a shrub. Sometimes, they just wanted to have their skills acknowledged. They were the Captain, after all.

'I've haven't had my coffee yet,' they warned. 'So if you could refrain from being overly positive while I settle in...'

Then Gren saw it.

The destruction.

It took several moments for their brain to process what their eyes were telling them. At one point, they nearly laughed, so ludicrous were the conclusions it was reaching.

Then they ran, stumbling, towards the navigation console, falling painfully to their knees. They barely noticed. Every nerve ending had been redirected to their current panic.

'No. No, no, no, no.'

The console which had housed AJ's physical form had been completely obliterated. Caved in and torn up, with a ferocity that had left behind a disquieting aura. Fragments of metal were littered over the deck. Gren caught a glimpse of a single rusted corner amongst the debris and was almost sick.

'What did they do to you? What the hell did they do to you?' Memories of harsh words exchanged crowbarred themselves into their mind until they thought

Fury saved them.

They scrambled to the other side of the console which seemed basically intact and flipped a switch.

'This is Captain Gren,' they said. 'Everyone – and I mean everyone – is to report to the bridge *now.*'

*

'We would be honoured to hear your song,' The Tooth purred. 'Will you require music?'

'I am the music,' Mel'Dee replied.

'Oh, well said.'

Flowerchild had moved to the edge of the ring and gestured for The Tooth to join her.

'We should wait for the others,' she mouthed.

'I'm sorry, my lady. Why is that?'

'They should witness this.'

The Tooth found himself irritated by Flowerchild's uncharacteristic vacillation.

'There's no need. Our deal with them was subterfuge.' He called to the patiently waiting singer. 'Apologies, my dear. We'll be with you momentarily.' Then he snapped at the woman whom until recently he had faithfully served. 'Or are you still hoping that your precious Bellboy will prevail? It seems a foolish wish. For someone in your condition.'

Perhaps realising that she was losing the high ground, Flowerchild demurred.

'Of course not. But they said there would be four singers. A group. Perhaps they've already waylaid the others.'

Mel'Dee piped up, having apparently overheard.

'I know of no other singers on Cinethon.'

'You see?' crowed The Tooth. 'The lies have flown in every direction.'

He marched back into the ring and, grabbing her shoulders, turned Mel'Dee to face her audience.

'Whenever you're ready, my dear. Show us what you're made of.'

*

Ella, Delios and Bellboy careened onto the bridge. There had been something about Gren's tone that told them, in no uncertain terms, that whatever had grown wrong had done so catastrophically.

'What is it?' Ella asked, breathless.

Gren, still prostrate in the wreckage, did not have to answer. The full horror of the attack was on display.

'They killed her,' they said. There was no sadness in the declaration. Grief would have to wait. This was the beginning of a promise that, in search of those who had robbed AJ of her life, everything might burn.

'Who, Gren?' asked Bellboy. 'Who did this?'

Gren reached wordlessly towards the undamaged side of the console and pressed a button.

A recording began to play over the ship's speakers. With growing revulsion, they listened to a replay of AJ's final moments in the universe.

And, from the first hummed note, grasped the terrible truth.

The Band had killed AJ.

Gren switched off the recording before the first blow fell. It was not something they felt they could relive and still survive to do what was now necessary.

'Where are they?' demanded Delios.

'I don't know,' said Gren. 'Along with... everything else, they've damaged the internal sensor array. They could have left the ship. Or they could be hiding somewhere on board.'

Ella had slumped to the deck, tears clouding her vision.

'I don't understand. Why would they do this?'

For that, Gren had an explanation.

'Killing AJ has put the ship into lockdown. They clearly don't want us going anywhere.'

'It's my fault. I pushed them too hard. They weren't ready.'

'Delios, you can't think like that. We all know who is truly responsible for this.'

Captain Gren scrambled to their feet, rage rolling out from her like heat.

'You can't pin everything on the damned Gods, Bellboy. Our arrogance is to blame for this. Look at us. A group of broken toys, messing about with time, with people's lives. Why? Because we think we know better.'

'Gren...'

'Shut up! We know nothing. And because of that, someone good and pure is dead.'

'You're right,' said Bellboy, to everyone's astonishment. 'Of course you're right. About all of it.' Then he reverted to type. 'Almost.'

A second murder felt imminent.

'Bellboy, don't,' said Delios.

'No, listen to me. We know *almost* nothing. But we do know one thing.'

'And what is that?' roared the grieving Captain.

'AJ wanted nothing more than to help people.'

'Don't you dare attempt to use her as some sort of rallying cry.'

'Am I wrong? Was that not her dearest wish? Every moment of every day?'

'It was.'

142

'Then whatever mistakes we've made, we need to do whatever we can to fix them. For AJ, if for no one else...'

He took them in, one by one. His friends. His crew. A group of broken toys, just as Gren had said. But not beyond repair.

'Forget the Gods. This isn't about them anymore.'

Anyone who maintained that modern villains no longer know how to make an entrance would have, at that moment, been made to feel a fool.

'Oh, we don't know about that,' said The Band, appearing in the bridge doorway, four evil grins on their four, apparently, evil faces.

Ella had to tackle Gren to the deck to prevent them from taking immediate and bloody revenge.

'Wait until we know what's happening,' she hissed as Gren struggled beneath her. 'Then I swear I'll hold them down for you.'

'We'd listen to her, Captain,' said The Band. 'You are currently trespassing on decidedly dangerous ground.'

Gren cursed and shook Ella off, withdrawing to a less tempting distance from their enemy.

'That's much better. Now, shall we start answering a few of your more pertinent questions?'

The Band clicked the fingers of one hand, the speakers flared back into life, and the sound of the Psychic Circus filled the bridge.

Chapter Ten

Musical taste is subjective, a fact well-known to everyone except critics and a certain flavour of terrible boyfriend. What floats one person's boat sinks another's battleship. The only true measure of a composition's success, when considered reasonably, is whether it has an effect on the listener.

Mel'Dee's song, by that criterion, was a smash. No one who heard it, that fateful day on Cinethon, failed to feel something. Unfortunately, what they felt was searing pain.

It began innocently enough. Her voice was uncommonly gorgeous, her delivery exquisite and the song itself a masterwork of interwoven melodies, countermelodies and harmonies. Sometimes it felt like an intimate performance, almost breathed directly into each listener's ears. At others, it rose and swooped like a choir.

But as it progressed, the volume increased, the tone intensified and the notes began to sharpen each other like knife blades clashing.

The audience beneath the Big Top began to groan in concert, which the song seemed to like, adopting and incorporating it into its own being.

'What's going on?' shouted Flowerchild, wincing and clutching protectively at her belly.

The Tooth shook his head wordlessly. Tears were streaming from his dark, cunning eyes.

*

On the bridge of the Vanguard, the effect was the same. If anything, The Band's condescending smirk made it worse.

And that was before they began to monologue.

'You did so well, Bellboy. So much better than the first time round.'

Bellboy let out a yell of pure frustration.

'You!'

'Us.'

'You won't get away with it!'

'Are we trading cliches now? At what point should we say: 'Mwah hah hah'?'

The music pitched upwards, keening now. Ella was sure her face was melting.

'Is someone going to explain what's happening?' she shouted.

'Bellboy was right all along!' This was Delios, his head thrown back in agony.

'About what?'

'About the Gods,' screamed Gren.

The Band clicked their fingers again and silence slid over the bridge like salt into a wound.

'Bellboy was right about almost nothing,' they insisted. 'But he was extremely useful.' Turning their attention to Delios, they cooed. 'Oh, my dear, you were so close to the answer. But like a typical poet, you had to overthink it.'

'You're the Gods of Ragnarok,' said Ella, understanding at last.

'We were.'

'Then who was that singing?'

'A piece of collateral damage.'

Bellboy began to laugh.

'Something funny?' said Gren, taken aback.

'Hysterical.'

'I'm feeling a little overwrought myself,' said Ella.

Bellboy walked right up to The Band and, for good measure, laughed again, directly in their faces.

'No, don't you get it? They're trapped. Whatever's happening on Cinethon right now, it's going to happen to them.'

'No,' The Band vowed. 'It isn't. Not this time.'

Delios gasped.

'It's not us you don't want anywhere near that audition. It's *you*.'

The Band acknowledged his realisation with a leer.

'Ah, the flipside. The benefit of a poet's imagination. Do carry on, Delios... see if you can figure it out. We're still in your mind. Exploit that connection and think. Think about everything you've experienced.'

Delios closed his eyes and concentrated.

'This isn't how any of this happened.'

'Yes!'

146

'The timeline wasn't broken when we started changing the past, it was broken when Gren and AJ crashed on Segonax.'

'Yes! Yes! Keep going!'

'The Gods were on Segonax.'

'Where we had been waiting for countless eons for... an associate to bring us the Circus.'

Bellboy wasn't having any of it.

'No. That's not right. You were always in control of the Circus. For years. I remember...'

'You remember... incorrectly. The Circus was made for us, was food for us, but we had no power over it until Segonax. Where you joined the Circus, Bellboy, you and Flowerchild. And where you both *died*.'

Delios' mind flooded with memories, his own and others, in multiple, often contradictory versions. But he was beginning to understand the pattern. He could see the truth, the original truth.

'And your ties to this universe were broken. By the Do...'

'By the Destroyer. That is his name. Yes. A fate we ought to have foreseen. And finally did, when this ship crashed on Segonax, throwing time into crisis. We saw what was coming and we acted.'

'You escaped on Gren's ship? With me? With us?'

'Not as such. We made use of the disruption and we fled. Into the past.'

'The Circus became yours across all time,' said Delios.

'We were *everywhere*. In all times, in all places. It was glorious. Until, that is, you and your friends

147

began to meddle. Time became unstable. *We* became unstable. And then there was an incident. A singer of rare natural power, bolstered by a psychic stimulation field.'

It was a monstrous sequence of events of which only Gods could conceive or approve. And only a man in a yellow military jacket and his friends could disrupt.

'If you want us to stop it, why have you kept us here?'

'Timing, Bellboy, is everything. You should know that. Here in this ship, we are protected. Shielded from causality. Able to reach out, continue to influence events, but unable to leave, thanks to the events now unfolding. Change them too soon, we remain trapped. But choose your moment perfectly and...'

The implication hit Bellboy with the force of an exploding star.

'You want us to help you.'

'Yes.'

'Why in the hell would we help *you*?'

The Band had been waiting for just such an opening.

'Because you have not begun to experience the cruelty of which we're capable. And you have so much to lose.'

*

The moans of torment echoed across the Big Top, merging with the music into a cacophony of sorrow. The audience had become a single mass, united in their distress.

148

'This isn't right,' yelled Flowerchild over the noise. 'We have to stop it.' She thought of her child, desperately hoping that her body was shielding them from the pain. And she thought of Bellboy, somewhere out there, somehow at the heart of all of this.

'My lady, no!' screeched The Tooth. 'You can't!' His face was distorted with agony. It seemed to be hitting him even harder than the rest. Perhaps, thought Flowerchild, it had amplified the pain he both carried and sought.

'I have to!' She summoned every shred of determination she had ever possessed, past and present, and placed one foot in front of the other. If anything could release them from this misery, she had to believe that it was love.

Love was all she had left.

*

Flowerchild found her way into the entrance tent, where her Delios lay crumpled, sweat coating his brow.

'The horror, intolerable,' he wailed. 'The humours ill, inexorable.'

She ran to him.

'Delios. Please. Sit up. You need to help me. Something is happening in there. It's hurting people.'

'Inflamed, in flames. In sacred flames.'

The poet struggled to move.

'There has to be something we can do.'

But Delios, Past Delios, seemed unable to summon the strength she needed.

'The ashes are upon us always.'

'Damn it, Delios.'

'I'm sorry,' said current Delios, pushing through the tent flap and followed by Bellboy and Ella. 'He can't help it.'

Flowerchild swallowed the inevitable questions. It was easier to just go with it at this stage. Instead, she ran into Bellboy's arms.

'I'm so sorry. I lied to you. This was the Gods' plan. I shouldn't have... I didn't know what else to do.'

Bellboy stroked her hair gently. He found himself reluctant to let her go. He hoped, when this was all over, he wouldn't have to.

'Trust me, we've all been at the Gods' mercy.'

'Do you understand what's going on? And, more importantly, can you stop it?'

'It's the stimulation field,' explained Ella, 'It's boosting everything. Including the Gods' power.'

'So what do we do?'

'We meddle,' said Bellboy. 'Delios, stay here and... look after yourself. Ella, Flowerchild. Come with me.'

*

Mel'Dee built to a crescendo that rent the Big Top in two, causing it to flap angrily above the now weeping audience.

The silence that followed was the slap after the slice.

The Tooth struggled to his feet.

'My dear,' he managed, though without his usual ebullience. 'I can confidently say that was a performance here that no one here will ever forget.'

The singer, who had been, until now, entirely lost to the music, became aware, for the first time, of the carnage surrounding her.

'What... happened?'

The Tooth limped towards her.

'A showstopper.'

Then from his pocket, he produced a tiny, flashing sphere. It ticked ominously.

*

When they reached the psychic stimulation field generator, it had turned against itself, possibly as an act of attrition. Wheels of errant electricity rose from its surface, chittering and fizzing. Circuits fried, rewired themselves and fried again. And, around it, an almost translucent wall of energy crackled menacingly.

'And this is what we meddle with,' said Bellboy.

'Is it supposed to be doing... that?'

'I think we can assume we've voided the warranty.'

'What's with the force field?' asked Flowerchild.

'It's protecting itself. Or the Gods are protecting it.'

'I thought they wanted us to help.'

'So they said. Naturally, I'm not inclined to take them at their word.'

'How,' asked Ella, 'are we going to get close enough to it to turn it off?'

Bellboy turned to Flowerchild and took her hands in his.

'Permission to take a silly risk?'

She bit her lip. He'd stop if she asked him. Somehow, she knew that. He'd let it all go. The world. The universe. Because she wanted him to.

'Just this once.'

'What?' said Ella. 'No. That's ridiculous.'

'What do you think I'm going to do?'

'I think you're going to try and walk through that force field on the grounds that it's only stupid thing we haven't tried today.'

'You really are a very clever young woman. But I don't plan to walk.'

Before Ella could say another word, Bellboy darted towards the force field and leapt. The two women half-expected, half-hoped that it would simply send him flying, bruised but no longer attempting to enforce his will on something as implacable as electricity.

It didn't. It resisted, but it wasn't as one-sided a contest as it should have been.

Bellboy let out a cry of pain. Flowerchild instinctively bolted towards him but Ella held her back.

'Your idiot, your *magnificent* idiot, might actually pull this off,' she said.

They watched in awe as Bellboy dug in his feet and, against the strictures of science and the warnings of myth, moved forward. One step at a time.

Which is when things began to get truly nuts.

Because as Bellboy pushed through the force field and closed on the misfiring stimulation device, bursts of song began to spill out of him. A verse here, a chorus there, never the same tune twice. Like a human radio station with a bored child's hand on its dial.

Finally, he was through. With a yell of triumph, he clenched his hand and put a fist-sized hole through the centre of the machine.

Ella and Flowerchild embraced, their laughter fuelled by relief, as Bellboy stumbled from the wreckage with a lopsided grin on his face.

'Listen to that,' said Flowerchild happily.

'Perfect silence,' confirmed Ella.

Talking like that, they really ought to have expected the explosion. It blossomed from the centre of the Big Top, flinging out a shockwave that knocked them off their feet. Flames rose into the sky, accompanied by plumes of thick, black smoke.

*

The Vanguard rocked as the blast waves reached it too, sending bodies and detritus flying.

The Band let out a scream of total victory. It echoed dissonantly from the metallic surfaces.

'What the hell was that?' asked Gren, cradling what felt like a broken arm and trying to regain an upright posture.

Then they looked at The Band and wished they'd held the question back.

They were splitting apart, the four bodies no longer content to share a single point in space and time. The faces stretched obscenely, like clay in the hands of an inebriated sculptor. The bodies bulged and twisted, fanning out like playing cards.

It was difficult to watch, so Gren didn't.

When it was over, there were four new individuals standing on the bridge of the Starship Vanguard. One of them, a young woman that Gren had no reason to recognise as Mel'Dee of Cinethon, briefly looked bemused before committing to unconsciousness.

The other three were the Gods of Ragnarok.

They had possessed many faces in their times, had been flesh and stone and air and fire. In this moment, all three appeared as tall, almost featureless humanoids, limbs wasted and angular, in tattered shifts of slate grey.

'We are released.'

'Free to roam.'

'Free to be entertained once more.'

It would be tempting to describe their voices as deep. And it would be true up to a point. But only if you were to content to describe the sun as warmish.

Mel'Dee stirred.

'Where am I?' she murmured.

Gren slid over to her and cradled her in their arms.

'It's all right, love. You were,' they searched feebly for a sensible explanation, 'part of an entity. But you're you again now. And they're them.' It wasn't getting any clearer for either of them. 'Look, just keep your head down. I'll explain everything the moment I understand it.'

'Gren?'

'You know me?'

'Of course I know you. You're the Captain.' A bolt of pain shot through the young singer. Her eyes widened in panic. 'Where are Bellboy and the others? Are they safe?'

'Sure, honey. They're safe. Safe as houses.'

'Did we beat the Gods?'

'You bet we did.'

'Good.' A terrible memory flashed through Mel'Dee's mind. 'Oh, Gren. They made me do things. Terrible things.'

Gren felt tears forming.

'I know. But it wasn't you. I know that too.'

'I promise it wasn't.'

'I believe you.'

Mel'Dee smiled weakly.

'It was good... to sing again.'

And then she was gone.

'You've killed her!' Gren roared. 'She was a part of you and you've killed her.'

'Do you know what it was like, being tethered to her softness, her weakness?'

'So many feelings.'

'Such fragility.'

Gren did their best to keep their temper in check. They had to stay on track. For AJ. For Mel'Dee. For everyone who had found themselves at the Gods' mercy.

'Look, Bellboy's done what he said he'd do. You're free. Now leave us alone.'

'No.'

'I don't think we will.'

'You challenged the Gods. You must pay.'

Those who had money on two Delioses[31] arriving at this stage should ring their bookies immediately.

'What say you, brother from the past, must we pay?' said present Delios.

---

31. This is, in fact, the correct plural noun. It is not, as some have suggested, Deliosi.

'What price and cause is it they claim?' countered his past self.

'What is this?' said one of the Gods.

'They say we owe them lives, for pain.'

'Yet without wounds, all life's in vain.'

'You say they owe us, for their skins?'

'I say we've shared communal sin.'

The Gods were beginning to become uneasy. Riffing has that effect on most creatures.

'What are you doing?'

'What do you hope to accomplish?'

But the Delioses were on fire now. They circled the Gods like predators toying with their prey.

'I've heard sin carries its own cost.'

'Death, I'm told. The winter frost.'

'Delios,' asked Gren. 'I know we've had our ups and downs but I'm sure you know what you're doing. Any chance you could make it so that I did as well?'

'The Gods have always loved a bit of entertainment,' he said, which was a good line but didn't, as far as Gren was concerned, count as an explanation. He returned his attention to his double.

'So, we agree, my brother from the past, the debt is due?'

Past Delios pretended to consider this.

'For all of us, that much is true.'

'Gren,' the first Delios asked. 'Do you trust me?'

'Do I have a choice?'

Delios' face lit up. He sounded almost joyful.

'Yes. That's the beauty of it.'

'What do I need to do?'

Bellboy, Ella and Flowerchild limped away from the ruins of the Psychic Circus, towards the Vanguard.

'All those people,' Flowerchild mourned. 'Just atoms. Stardust.' The Big Top had been completely destroyed, torn apart by The Tooth's bomb and ravaged by fire. They'd tried to get inside to search for survivors but it was impossible. The Gods had seen to that.

'We were a distraction,' said Ella.

'We were a back-up plan.'

'You knew?'

'I guessed. Thankfully.'

Flowerchild stopped walking. She'd recognised an undertone in Bellboy's voice that she didn't care for.

'What do you mean, thankfully?'

It was then that she heard another noise. Not an explosion this time. An implosion. A great, grasping hand dragging everything within its reach to a single compressed point. It was coming from the direction of the Vanguard.

'Bellboy, what have you done?'

He placed a calming hand on each of their shoulders.

'Delios took a message to Gren. A simple message although I'm sure he – they – dressed it up a little.'

'What was the message?'

'I asked him to overload the time-drive. That was the implosion we just heard.'

'Now I'm not an expert,' said Ella, 'but that sounds like a thing that you might usually try to avoid.'

'It is,' confirmed Bellboy. 'At all costs.'

'What about Gren and Delios?'

'Look, there isn't time to worry about that. Because the implosion is only the first part. The final reaction, when it reaches its zenith, will create a wave of temporal distortion that will destroy everything in its path. Possibly twice.'

'This isn't getting any better, Bellboy,' said Flowerchild with growing unease.

'And it won't. For the moment. Because *we're* in its path. Directly in its path.'

Chapter Eleven

A short note about voids.

If you have previously been told the sort of story in which a void is likely to make an appearance, or seen a void envisioned by one of the great holo-directors,[32] then you might think you have the measure of them.

The conundrum is that once you place anything or anyone into a void, it really ceases to *be* a void. So, in reality, most of the voids you've witnessed or had described to you are nothing of the sort. They're just big, empty spaces without furniture. The only material difference between them and an abandoned warehouse is the lack of rats.

And, in this case, the presence of Gods.

'Where are we?' asked Flowerchild.

'We aren't,' replied Delios.

Their voices echoed in the vastness, exactly as they would have done in an abandoned warehouse.

Flowerchild's hands flew to her stomach.

'The baby!'

---

32. See Rothchild J. Hawkes' acclaimed *Void* trilogy, for example.

'If appearances are to be believed,' Delios assured her, 'you are still expecting.'

'Take a breath everyone,' said Bellboy, with irritating casualness. 'We're somewhere else, I think. Outside of space and time.'

'What does that even mean?' asked Ella.

'I blew up the Vanguard,' replied Gren. Their own words sank in gradually. 'Damn it, Bellboy, I *blew up* the Vanguard.'

'You blew up a time-drive on a world being torn apart by Gods. It was the only way.'

'And you knew this was going to happen?' Ella was trying to make sense of the space in which they found themselves. They were standing on what she would normally refer to as the ground. But, at the same time, there was literally nothing to be seen in any direction, save the five of them.

'I had an inkling.'

'An *inkling*?'

'A strong inkling.'

'Are we dead?' asked Flowerchild. 'Because if we're dead, Bellboy, you and I are going to have words.'

'No,' said a God, 'You are not dead.'

'You are in our realm,' said another.

'And that is unacceptable,' concluded the third.

'Ah,' said Ella, unable to conjure anything wittier.

'I knew the Gods wouldn't allow themselves to be destroyed,' Bellboy said. 'They'd escaped through a rift in time before. I hoped they'd try the same trick twice.'

'And how did you know we'd be able to do the same thing?' asked Ella.

160

Bellboy leaned forward and kissed her tenderly on the forehead. She did not, as both of them half-expected, knock him out.

'Because of you.'

'Me?'

'I'm right, aren't I?' This was directed to the Gods of Ragnarok.

'You are.' It was a reluctant admission. Gods, on the whole did not care for being interrogated.

'You see, Ella, it was you all along.'

'What the hell did I do?'

'You set all this in motion.'

'I answered an invitation.'

The Gods, obviously feeling like guests at their own party, explained further.

'All would have played out differently without you.'

'You were the change.'

'You were the pivot point. The element we could not control. The circle squared.'

'But I'm nobody.'

'No, my sweet girl. You are most definitely *not* nobody.' Bellboy was beginning to enjoy his summing-up. He was back onstage again. Only this time, it was for one final performance.

'Flowerchild, why did you agree to the Gods' demands? Despite how much you hated them? Despite everything you felt for me?'

'For our child.'

'For our daughter.'

'Ella,' said Flowerchild, astonished.

'What?' asked Ella.

Bellboy addressed the Gods once more.

161

'This has happened before, hasn't it?'

'Yes.'

'The cycle repeated.'

'You sought our destruction, time and again. And achieved it. At the cost of everything. Your life. Ours. Your fury was unquenchable.'

'Your hate outweighed your love.'

'So you took a risk. Introduced Flowerchild into the mix. Thought I wouldn't be able to do what needed to be done if my child were involved.'

'It is a known weakness of mortals.'

'They enable their own obsolescence with such fervour.'

'It is most peculiar.'

'And, let me guess, every time I found her, I abandoned my friends and took her somewhere safe. A mining colony, perhaps. Where we died, leaving Ella alone.' Bellboy turned to his daughter. 'I'm so sorry.'

Ella hadn't been this mystified since the last time she'd been stuck in a mystical faux-void with some Old Gods, a poet, a bark-encrusted space captain and what she was slowly beginning to realise were her long lost parents.

'Sure. No problem.'

'You met your decreed fates,' said a God, in a tone that suggested they truly believed that should have been the end of the matter.

Gren rubbed their temples. They should never have become involved with time travel. Or space travel. Or walking too far in uncomfortable shoes.

'I have a headache.'

'There is no pain in the void.[33]

'You keep telling yourself that.'

'That didn't do it though,' Bellboy taunted their captors. 'Even with me out of the frame, you still ended up trapped in The Band of Infinite Harmony. Because Delios was as angry as I'd ever been.'

'With good reason, I'd like to stress,' said the poet.

'So you tried again and again. Introducing Flowerchild later and later in the timestream. That's why it seemed as if she'd vanished. We simply hadn't found her *this* time.'

'We gave her the Circus. Forced her to betray you.'

'But it didn't work. I always found a way to take her away from all this.'

'You did.'

'So you had to try something else. You skipped to the end. Sent Ella to Encore Station.'

'We thought your child grown – *with* you in the world, rather than simply as a concept – might temper you.'

'Instead, it gave me the strength to stay. Without even knowing she was mine, I felt it. I knew I had to protect her at all costs.'

'So it would seem.'

'Hold on,' Ella broke in. She was doing her best to catch up. 'You protected me by blowing everything up?'

'I'm sure he was doing what he thought best,' offered Flowerchild, without quite knowing why.'

'All right, Mum.'

---

33. God or no God, still not a void.

'No, that's not it at all. I took a chance. From love. Not hate. Because whatever happened, my family was not going to remain at the mercy of the Gods.'

'You blew everything up. You blew *me* up.' Ella pointed at Flowerchild's bump. 'Twice!'

'Can we talk about this later?'

'Fine. But it's going to be a hell of a conversation.'

The Gods were clearly not fans of mortal family dynamics. They interrupted impatiently.

'And now we have reached a stalemate.'

'You cannot stay in our realm.'

'You profane it.' But disgust soon gave way to a weary resignation. 'Yet neither can we destroy you here, without cutting our final ties to your universe.'

'Pretty sure that's on the cards anyway,' said Bellboy. 'You aren't really arguing from a position of strength.'

'Where there is time, there is... hope.'

'Finally, we agree on something. I assume you have a solution in mind?'

'The timelines you created have collapsed,' one of the Gods informed them.

'We must return to the beginning to prevent any of this from ever happening,' said another.

'Bloody time travel,' swore Ella.

'That,' Bellboy assured the deities, 'suits me fine.'

'Did you know,' asked the third God, 'that these would be the consequences of your actions?'

'Like I said, I had an inkling.'

'Has he always been this insufferable?' Ella asked Flowerchild.

'Shush, your father's working.'

'I also,' added Bellboy, 'have a suggestion.'

Chapter Twelve

Bellboy and Flowerchild ran across the dusty surface of Segonax, towards the first glimmer of hope either had experienced in some time.

Exhaustion was beginning to set in.

'It must be around here somewhere,' gasped Bellboy, as they stumbled to a halt.

'We're going in the wrong direction, Bellboy,' replied Flowerchild. 'They'll find us.'

'I'm telling you. That was a ship crashing.'

'I believe you. But do you think they won't have heard it too? That the kites won't find it before we do?'

'It's a ship. Transport. You said it yourself. We're the only ones left to fight. We get off-world, we find help.'

Flowerchild looked at him. Into him. And he felt the same combination of emotions she had always engendered. Love, yes. But also fear. Fear that he had led this extraordinary woman to her doom.

'How far are we going to get in a crashed ship?' she was asking him now.

'I'll fix...'

'No,' said a voice in his ear. Or possibly, his mind. 'She must go.'

'Actually,' Bellboy found himself saying, 'I think you should go. I'll lead them away, buy you some time.' He knew these were not his thoughts, that they were being fed to him somehow, but, at the same time, he knew that they were right.

'Me? Why?'

'She must be kept safe,' said a second voice. 'For the sake of the child.'

'I need to know you're both safe.'

'Both? What are you talking about?'

'She must trust you.' A third voice now.

'You have to trust me.'

Flowerchild bit her lip. Deep down, she knew what he was really asking of her. She didn't know why or what had changed so abruptly but she knew she did trust him. He might be the only person she had ever truly trusted.

She nodded and pulled him close. If she didn't now, she sensed, she would regret it ever after.

*

Ella kicked idly at the hull of the Vanguard. They were parked, rather than crashed, a generous but not overtaxing distance away.

'Oy!' said Gren. 'Mind the paintwork.'

'I'm sorry. It's just... how is this possibly going to work?'

'Your Dad made a deal.'

'With crazy Gods.'

166

Gren shrugged.

'He's *your* Dad.'

There was a long beep from Gren's pocket. They fished out their communicator and activated it.

'Yeah?'

'Can you explain to me again what we're doing here?' asked AJ, back to her usual perky self. Also, alive, which helped enormously.

'I told you, picking up a passenger.'

'Because of some guy called Bellboy that I've never met and a deal he made with some Gods.'

'Yes.'

'Sure. Why not?'

Ella shielded her eyes. There was movement from one of the nearby dunes.

'There she is.'

And there she was. Flowerchild stumbling over the crest of the hill, panting with effort. She caught sight of the Vanguard and shouted.

'Hello!'

'Hello yourself!' Gren bellowed.

'Are you in trouble? Is anyone hurt?'

Always ready to come to the rescue, thought Ella. Like any good Mum.

'We're fine! Just refuelling. You need a lift somewhere?'

'Yes! Yes, please!'

Flowerchild began to scramble down towards them.

'She'll want us to try and find him,' cautioned Ella.

'Lucky he left her a note then, isn't it?'

'And how do we know we won't just pop out of existence, like he did?'

'We don't. That's life for you. Besides, time ship. AJ reckons we can contain a paradox or two.'

Ella sighed.

'I wish he were here to see this.'

'There's always a sacrifice,' Gren reminded her. 'You know what Gods are like.'

'Unfortunately, yes.'

'But it was his choice. The older you get, the more you realise that's everything.'

Bellboy walked across the wastelands of Segonax, humming happily to himself. His heart felt deliriously light.

Above him, the kites began to circle again.

He simply smiled and waved.

When the car arrived, some minutes later, he did the same. Even when the door opened and the Chief Clown appeared, his painted white face laden with threat, the black of his tall undertaker's hat making a decent stab at draining the light from the sky above.

'Bellboy, you fool!' the Clown called. 'Did you really think you could escape your fate?'

'Oh,' Bellboy replied, picturing Flowerchild on some world far away from here, happy and safe, 'you'd be surprised.'

*

'Well, that's your mother squared away,' said Gren, as she and Ella made their way down the corridors of the, thanks to the Gods' reluctant but agreed upon rewrite of the timeline, not blown up Starship Vanguard. 'Just think, in eight months or so, you can babysit yourself.'

Despite have reset the course of events, Flowerchild was still pregnant, although less visibly so. Bellboy had insisted on it.

'Actually, I was thinking I might be too busy.'

'Doing what?'

'Well, it would be a shame to let the music die.'

'You want to keep the show going?'

Gren was stunned but not, to their own surprise, displeased at this idea.

'If you're up for it. No psychic stimulation fields this time though. We're going old school.'

'You mean I'd finally be able to eat breakfast without it turning into a novelty number?'

'Exactly. And I think I've already found us our first gig.'

As if on cue, AJ's voice came over the comms system.

'Call for you, Ella. From Othrys?'

'Excellent. Pipe it through.'

'Not,' said Gren, 'that I'm not enjoying this burst of new confidence, but you do remember that I'm the Captain, right?'

'Of course. I'm just the musical director.'

Delios' voice replaced AJ's.

'Hello?'

'Ah,' said Ella, in her best and most professional tones, 'High Poet Delios. How are you?'

'I am quite well. Am I speaking to...' There was a rustle of paper as the poet consulted his notes. '...Ella?'

'Yes. I take it you got my message.'

'I did. Although I'll admit to being a trifle confused. You represent a musical group?'

'I do.'

'And you want to come to Othrys?'

'If we're welcome.'

'Well, it's an unusual request, for us, but... excuse me, have we met? Your voice seems terribly familiar.'

Gren couldn't help but smile. Unbroken, untampered with Delios was still Delios.

'No,' said Ella, 'but I suspect we're going to be the best of friends.' She tried to imagine what Bellboy would think of her decision to carry on, to try and build something new out of everything they'd been through. He'd approve. She knew he would. 'Look, we're about a day out from Othrys, why don't we meet in person, discuss details?'

'Very well,' said High Poet Delios. 'In that case, I shall look forward to meeting you. May your travels be as free from care as they are full of joy.'

'Thank you, High Poet. Right back at you.'

The channel closed with a click.

'So, we're going to Othrys.'

'Only if you don't mind, Captain.'

Gren sighed.

'The show must go on, I suppose.'

'That's the spirit. In which case, Captain Gren, would you be so kind as to... take me to the bridge?'

~

By the Same Author

Acknowledgements

I would especially like to thank the wonderful Stephen Wyatt for trusting me with his Circus and Barnaby Eaton-Jones, Paul Andrews and the rest of the team at AUK Studios for trusting me with bringing it back to life.

Doctor Who has been a part of my life since I was a child. (Possibly, due to the vagaries of time travel, even before.) It has seen me through fair times and foul and continues to be one of my very favourite things. To take a turn in its playground, even at a remove, in the year of its 60th anniversary, has been an honour. It also very nearly impressed my children, Scarlet and Hero, who have shared my TARDIS journeys since they were much shorter and more prone to general stickiness.

To the splendid cast of the audio version of *Children of the Circus*, I owe a great debt. Not only for their electrifying performances, but also for striking the delicate balance of allowing me to feel like a grown-up professional while decidedly fulfilling a childhood dream.

Special thanks go to Christopher Guard for his beautiful songs and his enthusiastic support. And Sophie Aldred, for suggesting that Captain Gren might be gender neutral, a choice that really brought their character to life for me, both in the studio and on the page. Also Dee, Ian, Toyah, Wink, Barnaby, Kim, Other Ian and Greg, in addition to the above, for making the studio sessions a world of fun. And the rest of the returning cast of *The Greatest Show in the Galaxy*, scattered around the globe and, I can only assume, the universe, for making time for their cameo appearances.

I got to write words for Sylvester McCoy. That's not really an acknowledgement but I'm really looking forward to telling people. Repeatedly. When I wrote words for Colin Baker on *A Dozen Summers*, I never shut up about it.

And to Doctor Hannah-Marie Ita Straw who maintains she is not a real person and does not require acknowledgement but put up with a lot of typing and writing-related cursing when she was just trying to have a nice time.

You've read the book, now hear the full-cast
audio drama featuring the entire surviving cast of
The Greatest Show in the Galaxy

https://auk.direct/product/children-of-the-circus/

www.ingramcontent.com/pod-product-compliance
Lightning Source LLC
Chambersburg PA
CBHW011445170626
46816CB00008B/2522